Running From Fire

Legacy Series

Eric Hodgson

First published by E Hodgson

Copyright © 2024 E Hodgson

Running From Fire

Running From Fire is an extraction from the second book in the Legacy series. At the end of *Between the Storm and New York*, Frida leaves Berlin and sails to America.

1867. Frida Brant arrives in New York determined to make a new life for herself and her unborn baby. In her possession, 14 stolen diamonds. Hard on her heels, villains hell-bent on getting their hands on them.

After the American Civil War, New York entered an unparalleled era of wickedness. Criminal classes revelled in an orgy of vice and crime and the city deserved its title of 'the modern Gomorrah.'
(Herbert Asbury 1926).

The gas-lit streets of New York and the German and Irish criminal fraternities provide the backdrop for this fast-paced and violent historical thriller. For Frida, it was very much a case of, out of the frying pan….

4

Chapter 1

The little lady appeared to come alive.

As nervous hands removed her from the crate, the mood lifted. 'Look, see, no damage. Not stolen. Not just a pile of old bricks in there,' a forced laugh to hide his relief, 'I told you. You had nothing to worry about. Nothing.'

The sense of foreboding that had been eating away at Frida disappeared as the porcelain figurine met daylight for the first time in a month. Her apprehension had been contagious, but now the shipping agent wallowed in an air of self-assurance. As he rotated the small statue, brushing off the remaining sawdust, Frida's mind drifted back to Berlin.

Schmidt's downfall had been his tendency to show off.

The accountant should have guessed it hadn't been his looks or charm that had lured her into his bed. Had he thought less like a man, he would have concluded that this beautiful woman may have had a different reason for being there.

Revenge, perhaps?

No. The idea hadn't entered his head.

The diamonds, then?

She hadn't known about the diamonds until he climbed off her.

So, it had to be revenge.

But the arrogance of the man had swayed his thinking. The thing is, how could any woman resist the attentions of such a successful man?

Although he sat at the bureau with his back to her, he wanted her to see what he was doing. The fourteen perfectly cut, flawless stones, glistening in the oily light, bounced around on the shiny wooden surface, avoiding the tips of his fingers. A smug smile of satisfaction lightened his face. She couldn't see the smile; she could feel it… sense it. It rose from his nakedness as a shimmering haze.

To lay his hands on such wealth, a man had to be clever, cunning, and ruthless. My brain and your beauty… my God, lady, we could conquer the world.

This futile attempt to match his cleverness with her beauty and to make her aware of how he felt made him careless. Frida's only regret that morning was that the bastard had died happy.

The shipping agent coughed.

'Sorry.' Frida's eyes shifted from the statue, but she didn't move, stuck under the spell of those diamonds. What did he say? Speaking in English gave her a headache… she chose to say as little as possible.

He repeated. 'It says here that North German Lloyd has arranged a room for you at The Astor House.'

She looked at the man while studying his words in her mind, 'Ah, Norddeutscher Lloyd. The shipping company. I can see that I will need to work on my English.'

He smiled. 'We can send the statue on….'

'No.' Too abruptly. 'No, I do not want to… err, to put you to any trouble. If you have the documents, the proof of duty paid, I… I will take it now.'

'In that case, the clerk we've arranged to accompany you to the hotel can convey the item. Your paperwork and the bill of exchange are ready. Your cab awaits,' and he nodded towards the street. He noticed the questioning look. 'You'll have problems entering The Astor House as an unaccompanied young lady.' He slid the forms into a large envelope as he spoke. 'The Astor House is a fine establishment, the finest in New York, in fact. If you have

6

money, you stay at The Astor House. The working women of the area pester the guests, so the hotel will question you, embarrassingly, so I've heard. The clerk will accompany you and help you check in. He can carry your statue as he does so. The hotel porters will look after the rest of your luggage.'

Schmidt ironed the empty black velvet bag flat with a forefinger, pressing hard against the surface of the desk, checking for lumps, as if a fifteenth stone might miraculously materialise. Frida heard him snicker at his own stupidity. 'Two hundred and eighty thousand dollars.'

She wondered what two hundred and eighty thousand dollars could buy in America. The accountant had impressed her with his knowledge of the American financial markets, and she wondered if he, like her, planned to sail to New York. He was right; they would have made a successful couple had he not ordered the burning of Forester Street... the fire that killed Odette. Frida placed her left hand on his shoulder and peered over his head at the glistening diamonds, whispering. 'They are so beautiful.'

She pressed her naked stomach against his back, willing her unborn child to join her in the moment. Schmidt's heartbeat quickened as anticipation flooded his veins. She was sure her child's also quickened. His right hand dropped and moved around the back of her thigh. He sighed as he felt the smoothness.

The figurine wasn't heavy, even boxed up, but the clerk looked awkward carrying it through the grand lobby. Very business-like, he arranged for the porterage of Frida's luggage and helped her check in. The reception staff all spoke fluent German, but none interfered as the man conducted his task.

Odette's murderer felt no pain. It surprised Frida how easily the blade had sliced through his throat. Just a cough, some gurgling, and a torrent of blood. His head fell forward onto the diamonds as she slid her bloodied hand across her stomach. 'Don't be afraid, my little one.' Schmidt's dying had been far too quick, having wanted him to suffer, but she also hadn't wanted to fail. She pulled him upright into his chair, swung him around to face the bed and cleared the blood from his staring and uncomprehending eyes. *If that shocked you, you bastard, look at this.* She scooped up all fourteen diamonds, laid back on the bed and placed them in a pile on her blood-smeared stomach, in full view of her victim. His spirit left its pathetic body and filled the room, crammed every corner, permeated every space. She felt its presence as it crawled over every inch of her skin, and laughed at its helplessness, its inability to move either the wealth or the woman.

In Frida's suite, the clerk placed the figurine on the dressing table, adjusted the position, stepped back, and admired it. A thirty-inch Aphrodite upon a small plinth. 'It's a fine piece, but you know you could have purchased something very similar in New York and saved yourself a small fortune in carriage costs.'

She nodded in agreement, 'But this little lady holds many memories,' and placed a dollar piece in his hand. 'Aus sentimentalität.'

'Danka Schoen.'

'You speak German?'

'My family is from Hamburg. They brought me over as a kid.'

'I wouldn't have known, from your accent.'

'I do my best.

'So, you aspire to be American, not an immigrant?' Slightly puzzled, wondering why that mattered.

He held his head high. 'I like the Americans. Their patriotism. The immigrants are, mostly, disdainful of them, and distrustful of each other. They waste their lives hating everybody, jealous. And they're troublemakers, always beefing off about pay and stuff. It's much easier to get a job if you're an all-American boy. Anyway, all immigrants aspire to be Americans, even if they don't admit it. And they're stupid sons of bitches. You wait. You'll soon see the immigrant Irish battling against the American-born Irish on the streets. None of them seem to accept that the children of the immigrant Irish will be American born. The Germans aren't so bad, but I'd rather be American.'

'Maybe they just like a fight.'

He switched back to English, 'You're not wrong there, lady.' He reached for the door handle, but she stopped him.

'Hold it right there, buddy,' mimicking the language she'd heard on the docks. She eyed him up and down, liking what she saw. Scrawny, maybe twenty years old, or younger, but agreeably presented and confident. 'Are you attached? Single?'

His brow furrowed. 'Unattached.'

'Would you care to dine with me tonight, here, in the hotel dining room?'

He promptly switched from cocky to bashful, 'I, er....'

'Don't be shy. I won't eat you.'

He coloured up, and she laughed. 'What's your name?'

'Freddy.' He could hardly speak.

She waited.

'Drich.'

'Drich? Not very German,' sarcastically.

He shrugged. 'I call myself Drich. Should be Drechsler. Drich is German enough for my liking.'

'Well, Freddy Drich. I shall be in contact with your office and hire you for a month. I need somebody to show me around and help me with my English. So, call on me at seven this evening. If you don't make it, I'll have you fired.' She gave him a *do you understand* look.

Freddy nodded and did a rapid exit, almost falling down the grand staircase as anxiety took hold of him. Dining, surrounded by all those wealthy sons of bitches. Was his job worth it?

The luxurious finish of the suite impressed Frida as she strolled through it. She had paid the shipping company two hundred dollars to secure it for a month, hopefully enough time for her to arrange more permanent accommodation. Norddeutscher Lloyd had assured her that The Astor House was conveniently placed in the city, and comfortable. It was certainly comfortable. She buzzed for a bellhop and sent her request to the shipping agent for the services of Freddie Drich before setting herself at the writing bureau. She placed a sheet of the hotel stationary in front of her and put her thinking finger to her lips. After a moment, she smiled, then began her letter to Sophie Luxemburg back in Berlin. She wrote about the voyage to America and of her hopes in the new world, everything interesting, other than the murder of Rudolf Schmidt, and, of course, the diamonds. By the time she got to telling her about the hotel, dinnertime beckoned. She needed to remove the odours of the voyage and dress for Freddy Drich. Skinny Freddy Drich! She would sound him out over a hearty meal and a bottle of good wine, and if she detects just one cupful of what she was looking for, she vowed she'd knock the boy into shape.

*

A jittery Freddy turned up on the dot of seven o'clock, and he and Frida spent fifteen minutes together in the suite, calming the boy's nerves. They scrutinised the menu that Frida had had sent to the room, choosing what Freddy would ask for, and she instructing him how to conduct himself before and during the evening. He was a quick learner.

The dining room, on the first floor, was magnificent: high ceilings, enormous chandeliers, and the most elegant furnishings. There must have been two hundred and fifty diners, and the place was only half full. Following the maître d'hôtel, Freddy led his partner to the table and sat her before seating himself, perfect etiquette. Frida smiled and nodded.

'So, I'm your guide for four weeks.'

'Do you mind?'

He shook his head, and a thin, resigning smile appeared. 'Not really. I was anxious about eating amongst these people, getting everything right... you know.'

'You are doing fine. Anyway, you won't be just a guide. I need help with my English, with your American ways, and to help me settle. There will probably be things I haven't even thought of... dress, for example.'

Freddy looked confused.

'When I came through Castle Garden, even though they rushed me through, waiting to be processed, I had time to look upon all those thousands of people. I could tell who the Germans were straight away by their dress. I want to look like an American.'

Freddy laughed. 'So, you want to be American too?'

'Not necessarily, but I don't want to look like an immigrant. Will you be okay with the hours?'

'The hours?'

'Twenty-four a day. I can arrange a room for you on the top floor.'

'Here?'

Frida nodded. 'It's the servants' quarters, but it's still nice. How much do you earn in a week?'

He studied her and, for the first time, wondered how rich this woman was. 'Twenty-two dollars.'

'How about I give you an extra ten each week you work for me? I will provide your meals, and on top of what you are getting from your employer, that sounds to me like a deal. I'll also throw in a couple of suits, nice shoes, you know.'

'That's very generous.'

'So?'

'You don't need to go that far. Don't forget, Norddeutscher Lloyd will fire me if I don't accept.'

'Freddy, don't play hard to get. Do you want to help me out? I'm showing my gratitude if you do.'

'Don't worry, Ma'am, I'm teasing. It does sound like a good deal, and I'll be happy to oblige.'

Her smile was genuine. 'Good. First thing in the morning, I need to visit The Bank of New York and find out if Berlin has wired my money.'

Freddy took a deep breath. 'And what if it isn't there? I don't trust banks.'

'Then your services will no longer be required.'

They both ate in silence for a while. Frida broke it, 'Now, tell me all about the politics in this city….'

Notes on Chapter

Chapter 2

'Take my arm.'

Frida chuckled and slipped her hand through Freddy's arm. Yesterday, her attention had been on the little lady and the fortune buried inside her. She had taken little notice of the surroundings. Maybe it had been quieter yesterday? She was about to discover that New York was never quieter. All around her in the hotel reception, hustle and bustle. Porters pushing, pulling, and carrying. Gentlemen and ladies attired in the most elegant formal wear, the men bullishly scurrying about, the women more in control, strolling, gathering and talking. And, as Frida and Freddy walked down the hotel steps, out into the late summer sun, the streets and sidewalks, even busier. The brightness, the noise, the smells! The dreadful city smells, just like Berlin, overpowering any pleasant odours of sizzling foods. Huge, tall buildings hid the blue sky and cast their shadows, horse-drawn omnibuses and goods wagons jammed the streets, pedestrians… queuing or rushing about. Brightly dressed females, smiling at the passing males.

She stood and rotated slowly, amazed at the scale of everything. She remembered her first sight of Berlin. Apart from the smells, Berlin was nothing like this.

Freddy guided her southwards.

'You know the way to the bank?'

'Wall Street.'

Frida had heard of Wall Street. 'The Bank of New York?'

Freddy nodded. 'I'll show you the bars and music halls around Chinatown. As we pass through. We have time.'

Traffic choked every street. The sidewalks heaved with newsboys and food vendors. Shop windows with huge panes of glass displaying all manner of goods. 'Is there anything that you can't buy in this town?'

'You can buy anything, but first thing, you need to learn the basics about this city; everyone is after your money. Sell, swindle, or rob. And most of the time, you can't tell the difference. Watch out for pickpockets.'

'What about bankers?' A flutter of butterflies stirred the stomach as she asked the question.

'I don't know about bankers... or any of those financial folk. I've never had enough money to worry about that crowd. But if I had money, then I'd worry.'

As they made their way through Lower Manhattan, closer and closer to the bank, Frida's nervousness was turning into dread. Schmidt had said that her twelve thousand thaler would have been worth around eight thousand dollars. She thought about Freddy's income from the shipping company. Twenty-two dollars every week. Eight thousand dollars, seven years of salary. One thousand, plenty to buy a small city dwelling. Hopefully. God. She hoped her money was there. It was a lot of money. She almost tripped.

The Bank of New York rivalled The Astor House Hotel in architecture and vastness. Quietly spoken, private conversations combined and bounced around the panelled walls, making the place sound to Frida more like the noisy indoor food markets of Berlin rather than any bank she had previously experienced. Frida studied Freddy's face. As nervous as she was, he looked petrified. Her laugh made him angry, which amused her even more. The tellers sat behind their wooden counters, stoking the awful memories of how she felt when Gebhard von Blücher stole her money. They all looked busy, whether-or-not they had customers in attendance. She headed for the closest vacant position and waited for the man to raise his head.

Freddy pushed ahead of Frida. 'Miss Frida Brant, to meet Mister Harold D. Petty, Notary Public, at eleven am.'

The man glanced over the top of a pair of gold-rimmed glasses at the rude young man.

Freddy held his stare in assertive silence.

Then the teller sighed and stood. 'Wait here, please,' eyed Freddy up and down, then reluctantly added, 'Sir.'

Freddy smiled a smile of triumph at Frida and offered her the chair. About five minutes later, the teller returned. Apart from how he looked, he was a different man. 'Sir,' and he offered a hand. 'And Miss Brant. Please follow me.'

Freddy waited outside the office door.

When Frida reappeared, it was with a huge grin across her face. 'Time to buy us some suits and dresses, Mister.'

*

'Close your eyes.'

Frida did as she was told, allowing Freddy to lead her into the next street.

'Right. You can look now.'

In front of them was one of the biggest buildings she'd ever laid eyes on. Square. All marble and glass. 'What is it?'

'The Marble Dry Goods Palace.'

'A palace?'

'A dress shop.'

'A dress shop!' Inside, it seemed as big as Berlin.

'Eight floors, one and a half acres per floor.'

Frida giggled. 'To sell dresses?'

'Well, amongst other things.'

16

And so they shopped.

*

They returned to the hotel in time for afternoon tea, both looking splendid in new outfits.

They took comfortable seats in the cocktail lounge. 'You look a different person, Freddy Drich. Positively the successful young man.' She had been studying him. His manners good, seemed well-educated. Not that she was qualified to judge. Dainty sandwiches and sweetmeats appeared in front of them. 'Do you have ambition?'

He nodded. 'Every man has ambition.'

'Your father. Does he have ambition?'

'I meant every man of my age.'

'So, tell me. What's yours?'

'My age?'

'You are nineteen, twenty in November. No, your ambition.'

For a moment, he looked annoyed that she should be checking him out behind his back. Then, what did he care? He stroked his face and shrugged. 'Head clerk.'

'Rubbish.'

Rather arrogantly, 'I think a man's ambitions are his own, not dictated to him by others. And private, not to be bandied about on every occasion.'

'Because they are too outlandish?'

He smiled. Countering. 'Do you have ambition?'

'Of course. Mine is to climb as high as I can.'

'What does that mean?'

She shrugged. 'Take advantage of any situation that arises. Not to spend my life skivvying or working the mills, getting old before my time. Surely, you must dream of something more than being a departmental manager. You'll disappoint me if you don't.'

'Look, Ma'am….'

'Frida.'

'Ma'am.'

'Miss Brant then.'

'Miss Brant. My family is a poor family. I have two older brothers and two younger ones. My father and older ones are longshoremen. The younger ones….' It was his turn to shrug.

'Longshoremen?'

'Stevedores, dock workers.'

Frida didn't quite understand. 'If your family has three adults working, plus you, you cannot be so poor.'

'Applying your labours on the waterfront of New York City means you drink. Lots.'

'Oh. And you, do you…?'

A forced smile appeared across his face, along with a slow shake of the head. 'The wine, last night. It's something I seldom partake in. You ask about ambition. I dream of the day I'm no longer obliged to have to return to that stinking hovel and hand over every cent I earn.'

'Why do you feel obliged?'

'My mother is a good lady. She tries. And longshoremen full of whisky are not nice people.'

Frida softly laughed. 'I know what you mean about violent father and brothers….'

'I don't think so.'

'What do you mean by that?'

'Well. You're a fine lady, educated. You would not have turned out the way you have if you had had to endure the violence that exists in my house.'

Frida huffed. 'You have no idea, Freddy Drich. You really have no idea.'

He waited for her to elaborate.

She remained silent for the moment, feeling him examine her, looking for signs he could relate to. She was a woman; he was a man. But his examination wasn't the usual way men scrutinised. She felt his eyes dig deep inside her body, into her soul, and it intrigued her. And then she said something she had vowed never to speak of again. 'I killed my father and one of my brothers. Shot them clean between the eyes. And they deserved it; they were pigs. I ran away from them, escaped and went to Berlin. But they chased me, came after me. They wanted my money... wanted to control me... wanted to ruin my new life. So... I killed them both. There was no other way.' Her stomach dropped as she realised what she had just said. She felt as though she had dragged her entire past into this new future.

He bolted to attention, the piece of cake on its way to an open mouth halted in mid-air. 'You killed....'

She nodded. 'They were drunkards. Crude. Thieves and cut-throats. Made their money moving on stolen goods... and...' She was about to add, pimping her out, but restrained her stupid mouth.

'Sorry. I didn't know.'

'Why would you have any idea?' already regretting telling him about her past.

He shrugged. 'You just seem too nice. Sorry. You are nice. I didn't mean that.' Flustering.

Now Frida waited. Had she ruined what had seemed a pleasant relationship? 'I'm sorry, Freddy. I shouldn't have told you that.'

'I'm glad you did. I need to be doubly careful not to upset you.' He laughed.

The laugh relaxed Frida. A little. But she felt she needed to elaborate. As they sat in the corner in the comfortable setting of The Astor House Hotel's cocktail lounge, Frida told Freddy a very shortened version of her three years in Berlin, and how she ended up coming to New York. About the fire that destroyed her business and killed Odette, and the cholera that killed Polke. Polke, the father of the child inside her. Even she believed that lie. But not much else. Nothing about August Huth, about

Gebhard von Blücher. Nothing about Hasso Schinkel and her rise to the top of Berlin's vicious criminal gangs. She said as much as she could to make herself sound like a nice woman, rather than a cold-blooded murderer. The word, Claas, could never pass her lips. She never said how much she loved Odette... and she never mentioned Rudolf Schmidt! Freddy talked about his upbringing, what he remembered about his journey from Germany. About life for the poor in America. The war. The West. He wished he had the guts to walk away from his family. They talked until the restaurant staff made them feel uneasy.

Early evening, a tired but delighted Frida leaned back against the door of her suite and kicked off her shoes, feeling lucky about Freddy Drich entering her life. One shoe landed beneath the writing bureau on which the porcelain lady stood. The broken porcelain lady!

Notes on Chapter

Chapter 3

Her poor white right hand lay palm up on the bureau's surface, surrounded by a scattering of ceramic crumbs, broken at the wrist. The slightly bent forefinger beckoning help. Frida nervously laid the Greek Goddess on its back and cautiously traced her fingertips over the plinth, searching for signs of tampering.

With a sigh of relief, she placed the statue back in its position and sat on the chaise. What could she do with those stones? Leaving them inside the plinth of a cheap household ornament, alone in a room to which all manner of persons had access, was a recipe for a nervous breakdown. But to carry them about her person on the streets of a city populated by thieves and pickpockets wasn't an option, either. The bank? Gebhard's bank had strong-boxes in his vault, but she wasn't sure she could trust any banker after her dealings with that bastard. No, she needed to find a way of converting them into dollars, and the only way she could think of now was to find somebody who could supply her with the documentation that would make them legally hers.

She dropped back onto the bed. How the hell was she going to do that? Walk into a counterfeiter's premises and declare – I have two-hundred-and-eighty-thousand dollars' worth of stolen diamonds… make them legally mine. She bet Rudolf Schmidt had had it all worked out. Revenge could have waited until…. No. She had played it right, or as right as she could.

Tap, tap. A barely audible tap on the door. Standing in the corridor was a short, slightly tubby black girl wearing a chambermaid's outfit. Her mouth opened, but any words seemed to stick to the back of her tongue. She was clearly distressed.

Frida stuck her head past the threshold and checked the area. The girl was alone. 'Come in,' and stepped back to give her some space.

The chambermaid had a quick look around before entering and then, when inside, could not take her eyes off the damaged Aphrodite. Frida instantly guessed that the individual who had broken the little lady now stood before her.

The girl clumsily curtsied. 'Ma'am... I. I'm... It was me who broke the statue.' The flow of words gathered pace until Frida understood not one of them. 'Please, Ma'am, I have a child... I need to feed... I can't feed her if I ain't got no job to earn dollars to buy her food... Please don' tell them managers it was me. I'll do anything you ask, but please, I need this work...'

'Okay. Okay.' Struggling with the English. 'Slow down. Here. Sit here. Sit down here.' Frida splayed her hands and directed the girl toward the chaise.

Reluctantly, the girl sat. Beads of nervous sweat on her smooth forehead sparkled in the bright light of the gas mantle. Frida buzzed for a bellhop, which sent the girl into a frenzied panic.

'No, please, shush.' Frida put a finger to her lips. 'Come into the bedroom.'

The girl calmed and allowed herself to be manhandled into the adjoining room. When the bellhop arrived, Frida handed him a dime and told him to fetch Freddy Drich from the top floor. 'It's urgent.'

While they waited, Frida handed the girl a glass of cold water.

'I think this girl broke my little lady. But ask her, to make sure.'

The girl's untrusting black eyes bored into Freddy's face. Flee or strike out? She nodded her confession.

'Yes, she did it. I'll call the manager.'

'No.' Frida's left hand, open and hovering above the mop of coarse black hair, stopped the girl from rising. The other clasped Freddy's shirt sleeve, keeping him away from the door. 'Tell her it's okay. Tell her I don't care.'

'What? It's sentimental, all the way from Berlin.'

'Tell her, Freddy. Tell her we won't be involving the manager and that she won't be losing her job. Tell her. And tell her nicely.'

Frida sat beside the girl and took her hand. 'Translate when you need to,' she said to Freddy. 'What is your name?'

'Princess, Ma'am.'

Frida put on her kindest face. 'I used to work as a chambermaid, back in Berlin.'

Princess laughed nervously. 'No.' She shook her head vigorously. 'No, Ma'am, I don't believe you. Maidin' ain't no job for no wealthy white woman.'

'I've not always been wealthy; I've had to use all my brain and scheming prowess to get here. I'm going to ask, no, I'm going to tell the manager that nobody but you can service my suite. I'll tell them she is so good at her job, Princess is the only Astor House Hotel employee to be allowed into this room.'

Princess laughed again, but now it was a deep, genuine laugh.

'No. Don't laugh. Amongst many things, I've had to be brave to accumulate my wealth. You've been brave enough to knock on my door and admit that you broke the statue. I see a lot of me in you. I hope we can be friends.' Freddy had better translate this correctly, or she'd break his skull. And she told him as much.

A grateful Princess left Frida's suite. Freddy stared at Frida. 'I fail to understand. That *Little Lady* was the most precious item in the world yesterday. Now, it's what?'

'It's something a little glue can't put right. Go do whoever you need, to see and instruct the management of my wishes, about my suite being cleaned.'

'They are bound to ask why. What do I tell them?'

'Tell them I'm eccentric.'

'Maybe you are,' and he grunted as he left the room.

*

By the third week of Frida's hotel stay, she had found a property. A three-floor rowhouse with a basement on the edge of Greenwich Village, in Chelsea. She reached an agreement with the seller's lawyer to move in immediately and pay rent until the legal procedures were complete. Freehold, two thousand dollars.

Frida had found the house without the help of her loyal aide, and she felt a pang of guilt as she told him how she had gone behind his back. However, the property was to Freddy's liking, despite the sad face, and despite him trying to hide it. 'What do you think?' as she clung to his arm.

It wasn't his usual lovely smile as he nodded *enthusiastically*. 'Yeah, it's nice. Water closet. Lots of rooms.'

'Two water closets. Two bedrooms on the top floor with a water closet to share. I'm bagging the middle floor, though. It's like the suite in The Astor House,' and she allowed the pleasant shudder caused by the tingle down her spine to be visible. 'And we can all share the ground floor and basement. What do you think?'

Freddy stared at her, open-mouthed.

Frida couldn't hide her delight. She giggled in his face. 'Freddy Drich. Do you think that I'd send you back to your *family hovel*? To have those lovely new suits spoiled by your stevedore brothers. You can have a room on the top floor. Take your pick.'

'I. I can't. My brothers won't allow it.'

'They don't have a say in the matter. It's your life.'

'My mother will struggle.'

'Oh Freddy. You cannot spend the rest of your life living like that, worrying about your mother. She managed before you went to work. She'll manage again, you see.'

'And then there're my brothers. They'll come after me.'

'Allow me to deal with your brothers. Come on Freddy, move in with me.'

Freddy shifted into thoughtful mode. 'How much? The rent'

'Well,' and she rocked her shoulders and mocked disappointment. 'Thank you very much, Miss Brant. We'll talk about the rent later. If you can put up with an older woman running around in her undergarments, without a touch of rouge on her face, a room on the top floor is yours,'

Freddy blushed.

At last, a physical reaction. She had been flirting with him for two weeks without success. A game; attempts to force a response, to embarrass. Freddy Drich was too thin, too young, too plain, and not rich enough. But she had liked him from almost the moment they had met, partly because of his priggishness. 'I need you around. Please say you will move in.'

He pretended to consider the request, then allowed a broad grin to take over his face.

'I knew you couldn't resist me, Freddy Drich, mister-prim-and-proper. Come on.' She yanked at his arm and pulled him over the threshold. An onlooker would assume they were a newly acquainted couple, silly and playful. The gossips would consider Freddy a lucky so-and-so but attach a caveat – she'll hurt you in the long run; we know her type. 'I was thinking, if it's alright with you, to hire you from the shipping company for a further few weeks to help me furnish the place. We need to purchase beds, tables… in fact, everything. What do you think?'

'And a cot.'

Frida shuddered. 'Yes, and a cot. That's what I like about you, Freddy Drich; you have the uncanny ability to burst my happy little balloon at any time.'

'I don't mean to, Miss Brant. But you do need to think about it.'

'I have thought about it. I was thinking that it would be good to have you around. You could read up about delivering a baby.'

He pulled away from her, horrified at the thought.

And she burst out laughing. She couldn't speak. She laughed more every time she looked at him, tears streaming down her face. Then she stopped laughing, held a hand on her stomach and went down on one knee.

Freddy rushed forward, grabbing her shoulders. 'Miss Brant… are you okay?'

She couldn't keep it up and burst out laughing again. Rolled across the floor while he stood back, annoyed at being tricked again.

'That is a wicked thing to do, Miss Brant.'

'Oh, Freddy. Don't be such a bore,' as she rolled onto her knees and then stood, still finding it difficult to suppress the laugh as she brushed down her dress.

'One day, Miss Brant, you'll cry wolf once too often.'

'Okay, okay. I'm sorry. But you have to admit, it *was* funny.'

He turned away, and she stuck out her tongue at his back.

They toured the house, both excited by their plans.

When they reached the top floor, Freddy stopped and turned to face her. 'Seriously, Miss Brant, have you given the baby subject any thought? Tell me it's not my business if that's how you feel.'

'That's not how I feel. I have applied some time to thinking about it, and I'm not overly thrilled about giving birth to it or caring for it after it arrives.'

'How would Polke think about you, talking about his baby, if he knew what you were saying?'

'Polke liked his fun. Honestly? I think he would be less enthusiastic than I am.'

Freddy shook his head in disdain.

'But I have considered having somebody to cook, clean, and care for my baby.'

He shrugged. 'Yeah. Makes sense if you can afford it.' He scratched his head. 'I know little about these things, but there are agencies out there who specialise in housekeepers and cooks and workers like that.'

'How do you feel about Princess?'

'She's very young, also clumsy with it.'

'She's only ever broken Aphrodite. Do you know she has a child of her own?'

'Have you broached the subject… with her? Does she have a family? Just how old is she?'

'I've not asked her directly, but we have spoken. I've made a point of getting to know her. She's fourteen.'

'Fourteen!'

Frida nodded. 'Her child is just a few months old. She says she only knew the father for a few minutes.'

Freddy grimaced. 'Would you trust her, could you?'

'More than I would trust some Irish girl just off the boat. You don't mind that she's black?'

'No. Not at all. But I still say she's young.'

'But I believe she is very capable. Look Freddy, if you don't mind, I would like to further talk to her. I don't want to employ her and then have to fire her. That would devastate her, and she'd be in trouble. She has a good job at the moment.'

28

'I think she would be much safer working for you than The Astor House.'

'So, you don't mind me asking her?'

'No. Not at all. I think she would be perfect for the job, besides being young. I've heard that Negros grow up quicker than our women.'

Frida walked over and tapped him on the cheek. 'Thank you, Freddy. Now, which room do you want?'

'I like this one, overlooking the street.'

'But it's the smallest one.'

'Not much smaller, and there is only one of me.'

Frida smiled. 'I am so glad that it was you who carried my little lady to the Astor House,' and gave him a peck on the cheek.

*

The last day of Frida's Astor House stay eventually arrived. After checking the arrangements for the transit of items from the hotel to the house, she returned to her suite. Freddy and Princess were already there, wearing stupid grins on their faces.

'What's with you two?'

'Look around,' said Freddy. 'We have a surprise; can you see what it is?'

A little confused, a smiling Frida scanned the room. 'No, what is it? Tell me. I love surprises.'

'Give up? Show her Princess.'

Princess walked around the room, her shoulders rising and falling one after the other in time with her slow theatrical walk.

'She's getting warmer,' sang Freddy.

She stopped… held out her hands… and presented the surprise. *Dada*.

Frida turned cold. Sitting on the writing bureau was a shiny new Aphrodite!

Notes on Chapter

Chapter 4

The anger rose like an erupting volcano, only more destructive. Frida screamed.

Freddy and Princess cowered on the chaise lounge; *what the hell,* as the woman flung anything she could lay her hands on around the room.

'Missy Frida. Missy Frida.' Pleaded Princess. 'Missy Frida, they's is coming to the room.'

Freddy translated, 'Miss Brant, what is wrong? What have we done?'

'What's wrong? What's wrong?' she screamed. 'You stupid bastards,' sweeping an arm across the top of the writing bureau, sending everything on its surface to the floor, including the new statue of Aphrodite. 'Where is the statue?'

Neither of the pair answered.

'Where is it? Where is it?' and she jumped at Freddy, fists flying.

He couldn't hold her off. She straddled the poor man and landed blow after blow around his head and shoulders. Blood splattered across the chaise and over the wall behind. Princess jumped to her feet and managed to reach the door. She halted and looked back into the room at this mad woman, this woman whom she had given up her job for, pummelling Freddy's head. Two hotel employees raced towards the suite along the corridor, and Princess decided it was time to leave.

The two men pulled the still-screaming Frida from the battered Freddy. 'Did this man assault you, miss?' One held Frida back, his arms locked around her upper body. The other threw Freddy to the floor and gave him a hard kick on the head.

'What! Leave him alone.' She wriggled to free herself, but the grip was too firm. She lashed out with a foot and caught Freddy's assailant on the side of the ribs.

The man turned with a raised fist, but Frida's restrainer swung her away before he could get his blow in. Frida began to cry, and eventually, the man released his grip.

The two men looked at each other, not knowing what to say or how to react. 'Ma'am?'

Frida lowered herself onto the chair beside the bureau. 'Go. It's alright. I'll take care of Mister Drich. He's done nothing wrong. Please leave.'

Both men's eyes turned towards Freddy, lying on the floor.

Freddy, breathing hard, pushed himself into a sitting position. He nodded.

'If you're sure.' The two shuffled backwards, then turned and left the room.

Frida held her head in her hands, elbows resting on her knees, and sobbed.

Freddy stood. Unsteady on his feet, he went into Frida's bedroom, poured some cold water into the basin, and washed his face. He returned to Frida, knelt, and asked, 'What have we done?'

She pulled him to her. 'Oh, Freddy. Freddy, please forgive me,' she placed his face in her hands and gently kissed his wounds. 'Please forgive me.'

'I don't understand.'

'The statue has a quarter of a million dollars' worth of diamonds stuffed in its plinth.'

Freddy stopped breathing, then turned away and violently vomited across the carpeted floor.

'It's alright.' She took him into the bedroom and wiped him clean. His right ear was swelling. 'You didn't know. All we need to do is get the old one back.'

'Princess has it.' They both looked around the room. Where was Princess?

Freddy's hand still shook as he ran his fingers across his damaged face. She must have left.

'Where does she live?'

Freddy shook his head; she never said.

Nor did the hotel management know. Princess's old work colleagues pretended not to know; Freddy was sure of it.

'Where do poor black people live?'

Freddy had no idea, and he'd lived in the city the whole of his life.

It'll only cost if we get a result, was the detective's motto – or that's what it said over the door. 'So, you're looking for a black girl named Princess who lives in New York?' In a sarcastic tone.

Freddy felt stupid and shrugged. 'In a nutshell, yeah.'

'Well, we can't help ya. Best bet is to go see one of the drivers who cart them blacks into the city every day.'

Freddy went down to the waterfront and stood amongst the stalls of a fish market. Black women manned a few stands. 'Excuse me.'

She raised her eyes toward the voice.

'Can I ask you some questions?'

After a moment of contemplation, 'One question per fish.'

'What.'

'You buy a fish, and I'll answer a question.'

He sighed. 'How much does a fish cost?'

'Ten cents.'

'A dime. That's outrageous.'

'Please yerself.'

He sighed again and pulled out a dime. 'I'm looking for a young black girl, has a child. She's very poor. Any idea where I could start looking?'

'Wouldn't know.'

Frida had more luck. She watched the girls hop from the back of the wagon. They did it each daybreak at the foot of the steps of the hotel. The wagon hauled produce, and the three girls had been his only human passengers. She stood in front of the sweaty horse, forcing it to stop. The driver, old and white, swore.

Frida didn't have enough English words stored in her vocabulary but tried never-the-less. 'Can I ride beside you?'

'No, Ma'am, you cannot. Now get outa my way.' The Irish accent, difficult to understand.

She pulled a five-dollar bill from her purse.

The driver licked his lips. 'I have a load to drop off.'

'Good for you. I can ride beside you?'

He shifted over and she climbed aboard. He smelled bad, and Frida kept a distance between them while simultaneously trying not to alienate him.

'Where are we going?'

'To drop off the load.' He stuck a thumb over his shoulder.

The seat was hard, reminding her of the cart rides with Brant as a child. 'After you drop off your...' and she pointed a thumb at the load. 'Can I hire your... you and the wagon for the rest of the day?'

'Well,' he said, scratching his stubble. 'I have other clientele to consider.'

'That's a shame. Stop, and I'll get off.'

'Oh. But I'm sure they won't mind.'

Frida smiled to herself. 'How much do you charge?'

Dammit. He'd played it bad. 'I don't know. How much will you pay?'

'The five dollars?'

Five dollars was well above the odds for a day's work. 'Six…'

'I'll tell you what. You can have seven if you help me find what I'm looking for.'

He spat on his hand and held it out. 'Deal.'

Frida looked at the disgusting object, then placed her hand in it. 'Deal.'

They dropped his load at a yard somewhere in The Bowery, Frida attracting sideway glances, sitting atop the dirty cart.

'Where we goin?'

'You pick up the black girls in the morning and take them to The Astor House. I want to go to the place where you collect them from.'

'And you're gonna pay me seven dollars to do that?'

'I'll pay you seven dollars if we find the girl I'm looking for.'

'And how much if we don't find her?'

'Three dollars.'

'Five.'

'Three.' She guessed what the scoundrel was thinking: that he'd get the seven, and maybe more, whatever happened. She smiled at him, plunged her hand into the German pouch that hung from her neck, pulled out a large revolver, a Colt 1862, and placed it nonchalantly in her lap. Then she pulled out three dollars. 'There, take this. You get the other four when we find the girl.' The weapon returned to where it came from.

He gulped. They travelled north, making slow progress along a busy Broadway. As the congestion dissipated, the Irishman beat the horse, and the cart raced forward. They turned into a street lined by towering houses with doorways framed by columns and enormous windows. Street after street, the houses less and less grand, until the North River and Jersey cliffs came into view. The houses turned into stables, then iron-shuttered warehouses, until finally, hilly terrain with wooden shanties scattered about. 'What's this girl called?'

Frida's back hurt, and even talking was uncomfortable. 'Princess.'

He scratched his stubble again, a constant occurrence when he wasn't driving. He said nothing, just flicking the reins, and the cart jerked forward. They stopped at the bottom of a dirt track. He nodded, 'Up there, somewhere.'

Frida clambered from the vehicle, stretched, and rubbed her backside. 'How far?' He didn't answer. She tutted, turned, and walked. The shanties alongside the track were mostly in pairs, leaning against one another for support. Those not in pairs looked like rows of rooms joined to one another. She figured it would be a waste of time asking an adult for the whereabouts of Princess. She waited for a child to appear. A few did, wanting a closer look at the white woman who had business in their township. She beckoned to a girl of about eight or nine years old, who sidled over suspiciously. 'Hello. What is your name?'

'Angela.'

'Angela, that's a nice name. Would you like a dime, Angela?' Frida held the coin with two fingers and held it for all to see.

The little girl's eyes widened, and she nodded frantically.

'Can you tell me where Princess lives?'

Angela held out a tiny hand and led Frida further along the pathway until they reached a row of three houses. Princess stood at the entrance to the furthest one, holding a small bundle of a baby in her arms. She didn't look pleased to see Frida standing outside her home.

Frida smiled. 'Princess.'

'You stay away from me, you madwoman.'

Frida stepped forward, and as she did, two black men appeared from the adjoining room.

'Please, Princess. I am sorry. I didn't mean to frighten you. Please let me talk to you.'

'Why did you act so disrespectfully after what me and Freddy done for you? We wanted to say thank you, and you change into the devil. That is no way to carry on.'

'Please, Princess, please let me explain.'

'Missy Frida. There ain' nothin' you can say that could make me trust you again.'

You upset me because you threw away a quarter of a million dollars-worth of diamonds! Frida had thought about what to say on the bumpy journey here. 'My father was an evil man, Princess. On his deathbed, he cursed me. He cut off a part of himself and placed it inside the plinth of Aphrodite and said to me - this lady has to stay with me for the rest of my life. He said he'd seen a witch and said that if I became separated from the little lady, my firstborn child would be born without a mind.'

Princess held a hand to her mouth, horrified.

'Please, Princess. Help me find the old Aphrodite. Even if you don't return to my employment, like I want you to, please help me find the statue... for my child's sake. And she placed a hand on her stomach.'

'Missy Frida. I am so sorry.' She handed her baby to one of the men standing beside her. 'Come with me, and we'll get that lady back.' She approached Frida with a hand stretched out.

Friday took it and allowed Princess to pull her back down the pathway. A few hundred yards, they stopped in front of a larger hut, detached.

'Mister Ben, Mister Ben.' An ageing man appeared, wiping white clay from his hands. 'Mister Ben, what did you do with the old Aphrodite?'

'Why, threw it down by the water with all the other junk.'

37

'Mister Ben, can you show us?'

The man complained about being put out, but led them to the water's edge, anyway. 'Out there, somewhere.' Ahead of them, a mountain of broken items. Scores of kids scoured the area, looking for bits that might be worth a penny. Mister Ben gathered them around and spoke with them. A group ran off.

'What's happening?' Frida asked Princess.

'We have to wait.'

Ten minutes later, the kids returned carrying Aphrodite.

Frida beamed.

'You'll have to give them some money,' advised Princess.

'How much?'

'How much is it worth?'

*

Frida ordered the driver to drop them off on at the end of Broadway, on Union Street, and paid him his extra four dollars. It was a long walk; climbing down from that dirty cart would give the residents of this neighbourhood too much to gossip about. As they approached their new home, a gleeful Freddy bounded from the doorway and ran down the sidewalk to greet them. Laughing, he took the statue in his arms and kissed it and kissed it as he danced all the way back to the house.

'You white folks is all seriously crazy,' said Princess.

Notes on Chapter

Chapter 5

Frida and Freddy helped Princess climb the stairs to the top floor.

Tears formed as the girl laid her eyes on the room they had chosen for her, with its cot and bed, the wardrobe and dressing table, the massive mirror on the freshly painted wall and the woven rug which covered most of the floor. 'This is for me?'

Frida smiled. 'No, it is not for you. It *is* yours.'

'Oh, thank you. Thank you.' She lay little Courtney down in his cot. 'I cannot believe anybody could be so kind.'

Frida showed Princess the water closet and Freddy's room, 'Keep an eye on Courtney, Freddy,' and took the girl on a tour of the rest of the house. 'Now, you go and settle in your room with the baby. I need to talk to Freddy about business.'

Frida closed the door behind her and sat beside Freddy at the dining table. Aphrodite stood before them on the table top. It was a monumental moment, something Frida had been waiting to do for weeks. Now, it seemed more than she had in herself to reach out and touch the little lady. She touched Freddy's shoulder instead.

He took a deep breath, placed his hands around Aphrodite's buttocks, and gently laid the statuette onto her back. They both studied the plinth. He rolled her over. They scrutinised it from every angle. 'Are we going to open it?'

Frida nodded. 'I think it's time.'

Freddy left the room and went down to the basement, returning with a hammer and chisel. He rested the tool's cutting edge on where he thought the plinth might break in two and tapped the end. The base split... and a small black pouch came into view. Both sat, transfixed.

Freddy was first to speak. 'What happened to the man who gave you the diamonds?'

Frida glowered at him. 'What!'

Freddy shrugged. He thought it was a good question.

Frida picked up the pouch and rolled it between her fingertips, feeling the stones inside, the action producing a tremendous whole-body sensation, stimulating. With a deep breath, she untied the string and emptied the contents. Fourteen stones. Both looked in horror. Stones. Not diamonds. Stones!

Freddy jumped up and moved away, readying himself for a violent onslaught. It didn't materialise.

Frida just sat. Touched the objects, pushed them with the tips of her fingers. They didn't roll. Not like the diamonds Rudolf Schmidt had pushed around, anyway. 'I watched Fischer put the diamonds into the plinth. How did he deceive me?'

Sensing the violent reaction wasn't going to occur, Freddy sat back down beside her. He bagged the stones and pulled the statue to him. 'I'll repair this before Princess sees it. She'll have kittens, after what you told her.'

Frida grasped the bag. 'Good. You do that. I'll keep this, to give back to the bastard who stole the real ones.'

'Go back to Berlin?'

She gave a slow, thoughtful nod. 'I'll have to.'

'Who was he, this Fischer? The man who put the stones there?'

'Haus Fischer, a stonemason.'

'And you can find him?'

'I'll find the bastard if it's the last thing I do.'

*

The telegraph office on Wall Street seemed as big and busy as New York itself. Frida sat on a wooded bench waiting her turn. On the wall to the right of the waiting area was an enormous map of America, lines criss-crossing, connecting dots that were telegraph offices. Other arrows splayed out from a single point, this New York office, eastwards towards Europe. Her eyes focussed on the one with 'Germany' written at its arrowhead. At the front counter, which must have been fifty feet wide, officers were taking instruction from customers. Behind them, two rows of desks, eight in all. Directly behind them, a sea of desks occupied by men and women, two women, who, Frida assumed, converted words into Morse code. At the rear, a bank of chattering machines, some with operators wearing headsets over their ears, the rest with telegraph keys in front of them, busily tapping away.

It was a busy and clean office. However, unlike in Berlin, none wore uniforms, despite being smartly dressed. What was also noticeable, many wore the German style. The two females couldn't be mistaken for anything else other than German. Frida found the presence of her country folk comforting.

Frida's turn came around quickly. As luck had it, the officer was German. 'We can get your message to,' he looked at the name, 'to Fräulein Sophie Luxemburg. Is that the correct spelling?'

'Yes.'

'The message will arrive with Fräulein Luxemburg by this time tomorrow, at the latest. I'm afraid, as it's quite a long message, urgent you say, and sent during the daytime, it will be expensive.'

'How much?'

42

The man hemmed and hawed a bit. 'Three dollars, fifty-seven cents.'

'That's fine.' Frida looked up at the busy crowd of workers behind the counter and concluded that the telegraph industry must be a money-making industry.

*

She had been waiting for a long, long two weeks, beginning to think that Sophie hadn't received the telegram, when a loud knock rattled the door. 'Telegram Miss.'

She opened it and read: Haus Fischer left for America. His mother says Sunday 1st September. No more information.

Freddy had returned to the shipping company. While no longer receiving remuneration from Frida, his board and lodgings were free.

'Can you check passenger lists to see who has arrived in New York recently?'

'I can check Norddeutscher Lloyd's. Other companies… I probably can, but it'll take longer.'

'Haus Fischer left Germany five weeks ago.'

'So, he should be just arriving, or arrived. I'll check all ports. He could have gone to Boston, or Canada even.'

'But you can find out?'

'I'll do my best.'

Almost a week later, he arrived home with news. 'The port of Saint John in New Brunswick. The ship arrived last Friday. Interestingly, Haus Fischer boarded in Hamburg but didn't disembark in Canada. And even more interesting, the immigration authority processed a Charles Becker, and that name doesn't appear on the passenger list.'

'Canada. Is that good?'

'There are pros and cons. It's good for him in that it's easier to get through the immigration and customs process than here, less bureaucratic. Also, from there he can go anywhere. Worse for this guy, though, because of far less traffic, it's easier to check somebody's movements.'

'Can I get to New Brunswick?'

'Yeah, there is a ferry service. It takes less than two days to get there this time of the year.'

Frida ran a forefinger around the bottom half of her face. 'Would you like to come with me?'

'When?'

'Now. Or the next ferry, anyway. We'll get the cab to call in at your office and let them know I'm hiring you again for a week or two.'

'I'd better go pack, then.'

*

The next ferry out was ten o'clock the following day. Frida opted not to return to the house, and booked a night at the St. Nicholas, the most expensive hotel ever to be built in New York; it would be good to compare it with The Astor House.

Travelling light, the couple had opted to share an overnight bag. Freddy carried it into St. Nicholas, walking behind Frida. 'Miss Brant. You book us in. It'll do you good to practise your English.'

Frida nodded and approached the reception, smiling to herself. A man behind the desk looked up. She asked, 'Do you have a room for tonight?'

Freddy interrupted. 'Two rooms.'

'Freddy, darling, let us stop this silliness. A room. Please.' She could feel him turning red as inquisitive eyes landed on the poor boy. She continued the conversation with the receptionist. 'We only need a room, not a suite.

44

We'll be away at dawn tomorrow. And can we book for dinner this evening?'

The pair followed the porter up three flights of stairs and into their room.

Freddy looked at the bed. Big, but not big enough. 'We cannot share this bed, Miss Brant.'

'Of course we can. I'll have this side,' she walked to the far side, 'And you can have that side. I'll lay a towel along the middle. So long as you stay on that side, we'll get along fine.'

Freddy scowled but didn't give her the satisfaction of complaining further. He sat on a chair next to the window. 'Have you thought about how we might go about looking for this guy?'

'I would like to speak to the official who processed him. See if my description of Haus Fischer matches his description of Charles Becker. I need to confirm that we're chasing the right man. How do you think he got through using a false name?'

'A bribe, I should think. Assuming Fischer and Becker are one and the same, what next?'

'I don't know. If he manages to change the stones into money, or even just one of them, he'll stand out like a sore thumb on this continent full of poor people.'

Freddy raised his eyes. 'Did you know Fischer, back in Berlin? How did you meet him? Who put you onto him?'

Frida took a long look at her friend. 'In Berlin, you won't believe this but, just for a short while, I was kingpin of the city's underworld, head of the main criminal gangs. I knew people and I could get things done. Finding somebody like Haus Fischer wasn't difficult. I didn't know him personally nor have any idea what his pastimes were. I just knew people who knew him.' There was no way she was going to mention Neumann, for Freddy's sake.

'You are so full of surprises. Kingpin! Mister Big?'

'Don't mock, or I'll have you blown away.' However, there would be people she knew who knew Fischer. It might be worth trying Berlin again. 'You thought about a private investigator when we were looking for Princess. What about a private investigator? Look for a German named Becker who is spending lots of money somewhere in America.'

'That would be a big ask. The one I visited wasn't helpful, but we could try Pinkerton's. I've heard things about them. Actually, the name is Pinkerton's National Detective Agency, so if you are going national, they could be the ones.'

'So, using a detective *is* an option?'

'Before we go down that route, I'll go visit Norddeutscher Lloyd's office. What sort of reward could we offer for new information on the where-about of a Mister Charles Becker? How about twenty dollars?'

Frida thought that was about right, not too much to spook a person or attract too much attention. 'Thanks. While you do that, I'm going along to the public baths and have a soak. See if I can think of anything else.'

*

'Who is the biggest crook in New York?' She asked Freddy after they had taken their seats in the hotel's dining room.

Frida had given the search for Haus Fischer, aka Charles Becker, more consideration while soaking in the steam bath. The man would either need a counterfeiter to make the diamonds legal enough to sell on or sell them illegally, at a much lower value. Whichever choice he makes, eventually he would have to stick his head above the parapet. She needed an ear in that illicit market. She also had to consider that she might never find him. In that case, sooner-or-later she will have to forge a new career for herself in this new land, and she understood the workings of the criminal mind. She had contacts, like Neumann. It was an idea.

'Apparently, according to most people you speak to, it's John Morrissey, Congressman John Morrissey. Owns betting joints and casinos, shebeens, bars, and brothels… and a racecourse.'

'Sounds an interesting character. How did he get to be where he is?'

'Heavyweight champion of the world. Took his fists into the bars and made his way up from there. He's also known as Old Smoke. In a brawl in a bar in Lower Manhattan, a giant upended a brazier, then held Morrissey down on the hot coals as he beat him, but Morrissey fought his way on top and pummelled his opponent to death, his back still smoking away. But Morrissey is part of the Irish community, part of Tammany Hall. I really don't think a German would approach the Irish to trade stolen diamonds.'

'You seem to know a lot about him, this Morrissey?'

'Every New York American hates him and every New York Irishman loves him. He is the voice of the Irish.'

'Yeah, you're right. Anyway, I was thinking of somebody a little less public.'

'And a little less Irish. The dockworkers pay dues to their union; Irish, German, Italian, and my brothers are always complaining about the Turnverein, about them being crooked and corrupt. Well, I don't know about them being crooked, but it is an organisation with nation-wide connections. Who knows?'

'So I should join a gym club?'

'You could befriend somebody who partakes in their workers' rights movement. They are notoriously nosey.'

Frida pondered this. It would be a very long shot. 'Good idea.' Especially if she could get an introduction through Berlin. But that would be a dangerous move. That thought was not for Freddy.

After dinner, they returned to the room. Freddy visited the water closet. After a few minutes, still wearing his underwear and long woollen stockings, he shot from the room and jumped straight into his side of the bed.

Frida rolled her eyes. She slowly undressed, placing each layer on a neat pile on a chair. Naked, she then circumnavigated the room, turning down the lighting until, in the dark and wearing nothing other than a huge, mischievous grin, she climbed into her side.

A voice emerged from across the towel. 'I just remembered, on one crossing from Hamburg, customs processed a man with the same surname as yourself through Castle Garden, although nobody could find him on the passenger list, Claas Brant.'

Notes on Chapter

Chapter 6

Freddy opened his eyes, the room still cloaked in darkness, dawn yet to break. Sitting on one of the two hotel chairs was a fully dressed Frida. He rubbed his eyes and groaned, 'What time is it?'

'Getting on to six.'

'You're keen.'

'I didn't sleep.'

She sounded waspy, and Freddy decided it was best not to talk, just get himself dressed.

Conversation continued non-existent as they headed for the Old Slip Ferry on the East River Terminal, fighting against the tide of commuting workers entering the financial district of the city. The closer to the terminal, the greater the resistance, until they were fighting to just stand still. A well-dressed man dropped to his knees, hands gripping his privates, Frida screaming down at him. 'Keep your hands off my arse, you dirty bastard!'

'I thought you would like that.' Freddy wasn't laughing.

It had passed eight o'clock by the time they reached the ticket office.

Frida allowed Freddy to collect the tickets. She wasn't in any mood to play games, thinking about last night's sleeping arrangement.

'Rooms?' hissed Freddy. 'I'm afraid ferries don't have that luxury. It's communal sleeping on mattresses.

50

Segregated male and female areas. You can't spend while you're sleeping.'

The tickets had been ridiculously cheap, and Frida hadn't really expected private rooms. However, the on-board comfort and entertainment that revealed itself was a total surprise.

'The ferry companies are all straining to put each other out of business by encouraging travellers to ride *their* boat. Their key priority after getting people aboard is to give them the times of their lives, also known as separating passengers from their hard-earned cash. That's why they have the restaurants and the gambling tables and the bars. There is round-the-clock entertainment and a viewing deck with very comfortable seating – and stewards at your beck and call. The company doesn't encourage sleeping. Personally, I think I'll camp up on the viewing deck. There is a jazz ensemble playing this afternoon, and I'm told we can hear it over most of the ship.'

A glum-faced Frida followed him to the viewing deck. With an hour to go before sailing, most seats were empty. Freddy hadn't been wrong when he had described the comfort. Within minutes of settling, a steward carrying a silver tray took an order for two hearty German breakfasts. Nice. However, Freddy couldn't imagine thirty hours of travel lightening Frida's mood. What he had yet to learn was, the only predictable thing about Frida Brant is that she was unpredictable. Even docked, there was plenty of activity on view. The vessel was over two hundred feet long and a swarm of dock-workers loaded cartload after cartload of cargo. The sheer volume of goods loaded fascinated the pair, and Frida loosened up.

'Tell me about this passenger, Claas Brant.'

The question surprised Freddy. He'd forgotten about the man. 'What I said last night is what I know. The name appeared on the list of arrivals, but not on the passenger list.'

'When did he arrive?'

'I don't know. Obviously, recently. But I'll need to ask around for more details. Why? *Is* he related?'

'I hope not. Back in Berlin, I set out to kill my father and both my stepbrothers, but Claas got himself arrested for the murder of a man named Hasso Schinkel. So, he didn't die. I didn't get him. My father and Ode, my other stepbrother, were bad people. But Claas was in a league of his own. An evil son-of-a-bitch, in our American language. If he's escaped from prison and come after me...' she couldn't finish. 'Anyway, the news scares me.'

Freddy rubbed his chin. 'Maybe he hasn't come after you. He may have escaped and bolted for America just to evade justice. Maybe he doesn't know you are here. Maybe it's not even him.'

Frida pulled a face. That could be the case, but that was wishful thinking. Things had changed, and she couldn't afford to be complacent. 'When we get back to Chelsea, I'll write Berlin, see if he has absconded.'

'So, we live in Chelsea now, not posh Greenwich Village?'

'The wind is getting up,' changing the subject.

'Not too much, I hope. That Atlantic Ocean can be an inhospitable place for any ship, even hugging the coastline.'

'It's a big boat.'

'Yeah, you're right, don't worry, we'll be okay. The point I was trying to make was that if things get rough, we'll head for cover in a port, and that will lengthen the time of the journey.'

Frida shrugged. 'What will be, will be. It'll give us a chance to get to know each other better.'

Freddy grimaced. 'I can see that thought has put you in a better mood.' But he smiled as he said it.

Frida squeezed his knee and released the faintest of laughs. 'America is such a wonderful place, Freddy, so full of opportunities. After just a few weeks, I can see that New York is the place for a young child to grow up in. A place with a future. I won't allow some uneducated thug to spoil it.' She ran her hands across her stomach. It had been around four months since the meal with August Huth. 'It shouldn't be long before this little thing begins to wriggle and kick....'

'New York is great if you're wealthy.'

'That goes without saying. You make sure that, if you hear any mention of Claas Brant, you tell me. Don't respond to anyone referring to that name. Pretend you didn't hear. Just make sure you let me know, straight away.'

'You shot your father and his brother. Why can't you kill him?'

'I will Freddy, I will. But I'll need to take him by surprise. If it's the other way round... that doesn't bear thinking about.'

'Do you think he knows about the diamonds? He could have found out about them in Berlin.'

Frida closed her eyes and exhaled. 'I wouldn't have thought so. I didn't go round shouting about them. And there is no way Becker, or Fischer, or whatever he wants to call himself, would have announced he had them.'

'He could have put the word out that you had taken them with you to America, New York, even. That would have interested many people, not just your stepbrother. That would take any heat off Becker. What do they call a group of blood-thirsty-diamond-loving-thieves?'

Frida huffed. 'You certainly have a way of putting a girl at ease. But he'd be stupid if he did that. As soon as they discover I haven't got them, it'll be him they'd be hunting down.'

'Let's hope he ain't that stupid, then.'

The ship set sail, and two hours later it was pulling out of Lower Bay and rounding Breezy Point. The sky on the southern horizon loomed dark and menacing, and that and the high swell of the ocean kept passengers and deckhands in a pensive mood. Freddy and Frida watched quietly as the sky turned blacker and blacker and moved closer and closer. During the next couple of hours, most passengers left the top deck and retreated out of sight. Not seeing felt a better option. Frida preferred to stay where she was, and in control, or as in control as one could be during a storm. She could sense the ship being forced leftward as the wind increased in force, blowing the ship towards the shoreline. The noise was frightening; the stewards had disappeared. Then the ship did a choppy about turn, lurching away from the coast and driving into the wind, waves crashing over the bow and timbers creaking.

'What's happening Freddy? Talk me through it,' shouted Frida.

'I don't know.'

'But you work for a shipping line.'

'I sit behind a desk. I've never been aboard a ship in my life.'

'The way you talked….'

An elderly gentleman stood at the front of the viewing area, hanging onto a handrail that ran the width of the deck. He turned towards Freddy and excitedly, and loudly, interrupted, 'They're turning into the wind. It's safer for the ship.'

'He said they're turning into the wind. It's safer for the ship.' Translating.

The old man looked very much like he was enjoying the moment. 'They'll try to wait out the storm until the wind turns. I was in the navy before the war. Don't you worry, the captain will know what he's doing. They're up there now,' pointing upwards, 'working like Trojans to keep us afloat.' Just at that moment, a huge wave crashed over the bow of the ship and smashed across the deck window. The man stumbled backwards into the rows of seating, landing on his back, not far from the couple.

Frida got to him first, but both were there, kneeling beside the grinning casualty.

'That was a damn stupid thing to do, standing there like some land lubber.' He pushed himself up. 'They bolt the chairs to the deck, especially for times like this. We need to huddle down between them and sit on the floor. They'll protect us from flying objects and from being thrown all over the place.'

The three did just that, listening to the creaking and banging and crashing for the next three hours. The man liked to talk. Freddy translated when required, and Frida listened to tales of the old New York and unlikely sea adventures, until the tossing abated and the sun shone through the windows. 'We'll make a dash for it now, find a safe harbour before the tail gets us.'

'The tail?'

'We're in the eye of the storm I should think. The captain will build up a head of steam and go shoreward.' He enjoyed being the centre of attraction, especially when proved correct in his forecasting.

Nine hours into their journey, the boat dropped anchor in Jamaica Bay, behind Breezy Point. Breezy Point, where they had passed seven hours earlier. Sheltered from the storm, the entire ship relaxed, and the band played as food, drinks and gambling came back onto the menu.

The old man, '*Call me Jones*,' joined Frida and Freddy in the restaurant for dinner. 'This is what sea travel is about, the comfort and entertainment. Of course, I'm talking about peacetime.'

'You're retired now?' asked Frida, knowing the answer.

He laughed aloud. 'I'm obviously older than I look.'

'How do you pass the time?'

'Never took a wife, so I'm my own man. Well, I ride the waves… sometimes the rails, but that's not so comfortable. I might change tact after this experience, though,' and laughed. 'Investing is how I pass the time. I use up time and travelling, researching in things I might invest in.'

'Are you successful? Do you make money?'

He nodded. 'You know, I do alright… in general. It's a pastime as much as anything. A man needs to do things to keep this working.' He tapped his head. 'I could get one of them investment people to buy and sell for me, but then I would get bored to death with nothing to do. Anyway, I wouldn't trust any of them with your money, let alone mine.' He laughed at his little joke.

'Sir, you trade at the exchange?'

'I do. And on the curbside and in the coffee rooms.'

'Would you show me… teach me how to trade?'

'Well, I don't know. A woman….'

'I would like to know everything there is to know about trading stocks and your thoughts on the subject. I've seen things that interest me, as investment opportunities. I could pay you for the tuition.'

'Ma'am. It will be my pleasure to teach you everything there is to know about trading stocks and shares. It'll probably be the day after tomorrow before we get to Saint John, so we have time to kill. We'll chat for a few hours, and I'll decide if you have it in you to undertake entering such a rough-and-tumble world.'

They arrived at Saint John on day three in the late morning. It didn't take long for Freddy to find out which customs officer had processed Charles Becker. After speaking with him, it took even less time for Frida to establish that Charles Becker was indeed Haus Fischer, the man who had stolen her diamonds. 'Did he mention where he was headed?'

The customs officer shook his head. 'He didn't look the type to be travelling into the wild. If he was bound for anywhere other than staying in New Brunswick, and he did declare he wasn't meeting anybody, he'd have gone by ferry, to Portland probably, or New York. However, if it was me, after a long journey from Europe, I'd have booked myself into a good inn and rest up for a few days.'

Frida turned to her travel companion. 'Well, let's find ourselves a good inn. I could do with a proper rest and somewhere to clean up. We can spend a couple of days and nights looking out for Fischer. And it's cold. We didn't bring coats. We'll do some shopping.'

Freddy hailed a cab and threw the bag on board. 'I'll do the booking for the beds.'

Frida rolled her eyes as he pushed her aside and climbed aboard the trap. 'Please yourself.'

The port area of the city was busy and dirty. They looked across the sea of heads of scurrying workers and travellers. 'How the hell are we going to find him amongst all these?'

'I reckon New York was like this, before it became modern.'

The low grey sky enveloped the city, and mules and horses steamed from pulling their loads through the muddy streets. It didn't look an inviting sort of place. 'If I was Becker, I'm not sure that I'd have stayed for too long, if at all. I'd head for just about anywhere other than New York.'

Despite anticipating his reason for saying it, Frida asked, 'Why not New York?'

'Because that's where you said you were going.'

'But I didn't. I told him I was bound for Chicago. I was carrying a quarter of a million dollars' worth of diamonds. I'm not that stupid.'

'So, we look everywhere other than Chicago?'

Frida detected a hint of sarcasm. 'Unless he thinks I was bluffing. Anyway, if you think that thought is bad enough, he'll probably change his name again. I would.'

Freddy gave up and dropped his eyes downwards.

Notes on Chapter

Chapter 7

In the end, the pair decided against staying over in Saint John. Their cab pulled up outside Frida's house in Union Street, three long and arduous days after leaving Canada, travelling by steamboat to Portland, then across country, via Boston, by rail.

The weeks went by. There was no sign of Claas and no news of Charles Becker, or Haus Fischer, or whatever tag the man had hung around his neck. Frida grew bigger and bigger.

She liked the old man, *call me Jones*. He visited infrequently to begin with, but as time moved on, more regularly. In the early days, Freddy would join them, serving as a translator. However, as Frida's English language skills improved, Freddy's help became less necessary, much to his disappointment. Frida attributed his discontent to jealousy, and Frida, being Frida, teased Freddy by being overly flirtatious with the old man. Behind Freddy's back, Frida and Princess laughed about the boy's behaviour, especially towards her flirting with a man of Jones's age, with his difficulty of mobility.

Then, one day, Princess changed her attitude. 'Missy Frida, that boy's not jealous, he is worried. That ol' man is a scary con artist, an' he's going to separate you from your money an' we'll all be walking the streets without shoes on our feet.'

Frida laughed. This was a new tactic. 'Freddy's been working on you, Princess. You tell him to mind his own business and to behave himself towards my guest.'

Princess turned and tutted her way back up the stairs, shaking her head like a disagreeable old maid.

Jones had told Frida all about the bucket shops, pump and dump schemes, churning, misrepresentation, forgery, and front running. Market manipulation tactics and fraudulent activities she would be proud to use. No, Jones was looking after her interests, making sure that she would see a con when she saw one. *He was as straight as a die.* Anyway, she had, as yet, to invest any funds.

Jones accompanied her, early one wintery morning, to the new stock exchange building on Broad Street. He directed her through swirling sleet into a building opposite the exchange, up to a first-floor office of an acquaintance. Around a dozen men stood idly around, and they stepped back to allow Jones to place a chair by the window overlooking the street. 'Sit here, Miss Brant, and you can watch the workings of the curbstone dealers.'

The window was icy, and a sprinkling of snow had settled; she couldn't see much and she figured the room's occupants would not appreciate an open window.

'Don't you worry. When the time comes, I can assure you, that window will be open.' The old man passed her a mug of bitter coffee and stood behind her. As the liquid steamed in her hands, she watched the men. They were all dressed for the wintery conditions, but here, out of the clutches of the freezing wind, a cloud of warmth hovered above their reddening heads. Some stood alone, studying notes. Many were in pairs, in deep whispered conversation, often looking in her direction as they listened to the mouth in their ear. A feeling of paranoia rose, and Jones interpreted her glance as a call for help.

'I can assure you, my dear, despite looking in the direction of the rare appearance of a female in the vicinity, even one as pretty as yourself, the minds of these gentlemen will be firmly on the day's proceedings.'

The words were only mildly comforting. Polke's little so-and-so was at a stage where it seemed to relish keeping Frida awake all night, with its kicking and constant manoeuvring. The lack of a proper night's sleep was taking its toll. Her back ached, and she felt weary and heavy… fat even. And the constant need to visit the bathroom added to the discomfort. The water closet, Jones's friend apologised, was not the most eloquent, although she'd seen worse. Despite it being she who had persuaded Jones to bring her along, she wasn't enjoying the experience; she wasn't feeling at all attractive.

When she reappeared for the second or third time, the room had almost emptied, replaced by icy gusts with razor-sharp edges from the open window. Despite the urge to remove the weight from her feet, the chair now looked uninviting. However, she found it too wearing, remaining on her feet, and the moment she sat she forgot all about her discomforts.

There must have been a thousand men, more, covering the sidewalks and the street. As far as she could see, men followed the street's activities from open windows, signalling with waving arms and pointing fingers. They handed notes down to young boys, who raced off in all directions. Chalk boards, with words and figures frantically added, altered, and rubbed out. And the noise! The inclement weather forgotten. The scene pulled her like a magnet and Jones had to almost restrain her from sliding through the frame of the window.

A man squeezed beside her, watched what she was watching, but observed different things… he turned, 'York Steel down fourteen cents!'

'Buy. Ten thousand,' came the reply from behind a serving hatch at the back of the office, and the man returned his face to the street and nodded three times. For the first time Frida noticed the plethora of wires criss-crossing the street, along which she imagined world-wide news of natural disasters, the progress of wars, government announcement, and of new inventions and the deaths of kings racing right into the busy offices along Broad Street. Events that affected the actions of the traders. But it wasn't only world events that influenced. Other traders' activities seemed to play as big a part in swaying decisions.

Boys raced noisily up the stairs and planted notes into hands behind the hatch, and from there, instructions flew into the cauldron below, via the man next to Frida. The heavily pregnant German felt as if was her being reborn. This was her new world, and she vowed to join it and conquer it.

The excursion took its toll. Frida returned home exhausted, in no mood to defend herself, on the receiving end of a scolding from Princess. Employing the girl had turned out to be a stroke of good fortune. Her knowledge of caring for a woman during pregnancy was second to none, despite her tender age and, during the final two months prior to the birth, Frida needed Princess. Tiring and messy, sleepless nights, listless days, swollen and painful joints, and continuous heartburn and false contractions. Why do women allow themselves to be put through this?

During a vicious snowstorm on the afternoon of Saint Valentine's Day in 1868, Nathanial Brant entered the world. The pregnancy had been difficult, but the birth brought with it a rush of emotions too wonderful to describe, and those terrible few months pushed onto the back burner. As she held her baby boy against her breast, his fretful cries turned into a contented gurgle, and Frida cried.

Freddy feigned disinterest, but Frida could tell that he took more than a passing interest in her child. More than once, she found him smiling and cooing into the cot. This display of love from someone who seemed to find it hard to display his feelings deeply touched Frida, to where she felt sorry for teasing the boy. She would try her hardest to stop.

By May, when Nathen was getting bigger and heavier by the minute, 'Call me Jones' reappeared. Much to the displeasure of Freddy and Princess. They had assumed that motherhood had replaced Frida's urge to be drawn into that *man's world*. But, as they say, a leopard cannot change its spots. The frequency of the old man's visits returned to pre-Nathan times, but now with more urgent, one-sided monologues. Less teaching, more persuasion. Generally, Freddy was at work, and it left Princess alone to show her disapproval. In the end, Frida barred her from being present during these business meeting, other than the serving of beverages.

'A new company, Philadelphia Telegraph. Two bankrupt businesses merged and forming one, with new investors in place. Philadelphia's financial district is mushrooming. It's the place to invest.'

Frida had, over the months, and as a tool to help her English, become an avid reader of the city's prominent newspapers, The Times, Herald, Tribune, and World. Even various New York Journals could be found stacked in the corner. Many writers had written countless positive words about Philadelphia's financial importance to the American economy, specifically praising the class and quality of the investors. Fools and scoundrels were hard to find there, unlike in New York. Almost every word about Philadelphia was encouraging. And, to be honest, if they had not been, Frida would have ignored them.

Before Jones's next visit, Frida deliberated. He had suggested five hundred dollars, and that it should be cash. When he next entered the house, ten fifty-dollar bills awaited him. By the time the sun was warm, and Nathan was mimicking sounds, the investment had grown to over thirteen hundred dollars.

Princess delivered tea with a beaming false smile.

Frida scowled.

Jones sat back, oblivious to the maid's feelings. 'Time to cash in, I think.'

Frida sat up. 'No, surely not. While we are doing so well?'

'It's time. I'll drop the cash off as soon as I have it.'

Frida looked disappointed.

'Well.' A thoughtful Jones rubbed his stubbled chin. 'There is another opportunity surfacing. A businessman named Andrew Carnegie is on the lookout for partners, but it will cost four thousand.'

Andrew Carnegie. Steel. Frida had read about him. 'What is your advice, sir?'

'Well, it's a lot of money. However, if this venture works as well as his other ventures, we could be looking at a substantial profit.'

Frida shook her head. 'Four thousand is too much money.'

'You already have thirteen hundred. I would invest the entire four myself, but I've tied most of my money up in other investments, but,' he scratched that chin again, 'we could go in together. I could afford a thousand bucks.'

Frida exhaled a long, reflective breath. 'That leaves one thousand, seven hundred... okay. Cash?'

Jones nodded. 'Are you sure?'

'Let us go for it. I trust you, Sir, especially as you will also be risking your own money.'

Jones adopted his fatherly stance. 'You must not stretch yourself too much. Are you sure you can afford it?'

Frida smiled. 'Thank you for caring, but there is plenty more where that comes from. My problem is a faint heart, not a lack of funds. Perhaps when I have experienced a few more good days.... No. We will pop down to Wall

Street and collect some more of those greenbacks. Let us strike while the iron is hot.'

'My God, young lady, forget the faint heart. You have nerves of steel.'

Later that evening, Freddy, hot from the shipping company offices, burst into the sitting room, a huffing and puffing Princess close on his heels. 'Are you mad?'

Frida scowled. 'I see you and that nosey maid have been discussing my affairs.'

'That man, Jones, if that really is his name, is wringing you dry. Why can't you see that?'

Frida turned to Princess. 'Did you listen in on our private conversation?'

The girl didn't need to turn red; guilt written all over her face.

Frida shouted. 'Get out!'

'It's your interests we're looking after,' quipped Freddy.

Frida growled. 'And I will not tell you again. It is my business… not yours.'

'It'll be our business if we all end up on the street.'

'I will tell you, just once more, Freddy. Mind your own business.'

'Well, I refuse to stand by and watch that conman take your money.'

'Okay.' Frida shrugged, 'go then. Get out.'

Freddy reversed past Princess, turned, and almost slammed the door off its hinges as he left. Princess held a hand to her mouth to stifle a cry as she followed him.

Frida sighed. She could hear the pair talking from the top floor, then they rushed down the stairs, and Freddy fell out into the street.

Princess hesitantly opened the door and poked her head into the room. 'Freddy has gone.'

Frida gave a nonchalant shrug. 'He will be back.'

But he didn't return, and for the next couple of months, a cloud of gloom hung over the house. Only the encouraging updates about her investment and Nathan's hilarious attempts to eat solid food kept the household from total despair.

And then the day Frida was waiting for arrived. It was a hot, early September day, when Princess announced the arrival of a sweating Jones. 'Mr Jones. How are you, Sir? Come, sit, have a cold drink.'

Jones sat.

'Have you news of our investments?'

He wiped his forehead and loosened the bow tie. 'My dear. Wonderful news. We've had an offer of eight thousand dollars for our holding in Andrew Carnegie's project. Double what we invested.'

Frida jumped up and down with delight. 'That is wonderful, Sir. Do we accept?'

'Normally, I would say no. But there's another opportunity, an even more promising one. The choice is yours.'

Frida raised her hands to her face. 'Really. Tell me.'

'Cornelius Vanderbilt?'

'Yes. Everybody knows of Cornelius Vanderbilt.'

'Well, I can tell you, he is looking for investments for The New York Central Railroad. It's a similar deal to the one with Andrew Carnegie. An opportunity has come my way, to gather a group of investors, to raise funds and take part.'

'How many investors?'

'Twenty, probably. It depends on how much each one is prepared to cough up.'

'Twenty. That's too many. I do not like that. How much are you looking for?'

Jones pulled a face, as if too embarrassed to say. 'One hundred thousand dollars.'

'Wow. And how many people are interested?'

'You are the first I've spoken to. But I don't think I'll have a problem finding others. It's a deal that doesn't come around often. So, it won't disappoint me if you decline. I understand your reluctance.'

Frida sat back and linked her fingers behind her head and sucked air. 'I will put up all the money.'

Jones almost choked. 'All! All of it?'

'Yes. I think I could manage it. It will require a few days to organise. How soon do you need it?'

Jones stared at her with an open mouth. 'Are you serious?'

Frida nodded.

'Eight... nine days. As long as they know it's on its way. Possibly two weeks.'

'It can be cash, but you will have to collect it from the Bank of New York, with security. One hundred thousand dollars is a lot of money.'

The old man was astounded. 'Yes. One hundred thousand dollars is a lot of money.' He was about to add something when she interrupted.

'There is just one thing. I trust you very much. But I would like my share of the Andrew Carnegie holding first, in cash. We have been investing for six months now, and it would be nice to feel the profit.'

'Of course, my dear, I'll bring it to you at the end of the week. It will be around six thousand. Miss Brant, you are full of surprises.'

*

The two met in the foyer of the Bank of New York, and Jones handed her six thousand, one hundred and forty dollars. The teller was all smiles as he entered it into her account. Jones looked uncomfortable, and Frida smiled to herself.

'Let me buy you dinner, Mr Jones. I have heard of a little restaurant on the Hudson River waterfront.'

'I would love dinner, but are you sure about the waterfront? It can be an uninviting place.'

'Uninviting. No. Not at all. I have been there frequently.'

Jones was confused, but he climbed aboard a cab. The ride took about ten muted minutes, until it pulled up in front of a poorly decorated boarding house. Frida smiled, and they both alighted.

'What… what are we doing here?'

Frida laughed. 'You might ask, is this not where you sleep?'

The cab pulled away.

'I… I don't understand.'

'Follow me, Mr Jones.' She led him away from the boarding house, toward the water's edge. The Hudson River moved slowly and murky, but still glistened under the mid-day sun. The constant hammering and clattering from the close-by docks was the only thing spoiling the moment.

It wasn't a long walk; however, Jones was breathless as they reached a wooden jetty. 'What are we doing, Miss Brant?'

'You know, Mr Jones, we have known each other for a while now, yet I feel as though you are keeping things from me. Like, where did you lay your hands on six thousand dollars?'

'Well, you know where.'

'But I don't, Sir. You should have chosen a better vehicle than Philadelphia Telegraph to relieve me of my cash. It doesn't exist. Do you really think I would hand over five hundred dollars without doing my own digging around? And likewise, there was no Andrew Carnegie Fund… and no *Mister Jones*. I've not even bothered to check out this… this Vanderbilt opportunity. The things I don't know, and would like you to tell me are, after handing you two thousand, two hundred dollars, how you were able to hand over than six thousand back, who gave you the cash, and, why me? What made you choose me on that boat trip to Saint John?'

Jones turned his back on her and looked upriver.

Frida could tell by his shoulder movement that he had slipped a hand inside his jacket. The nozzle of a Colt 1680 dug into the back of his head. 'Take your hand away from that pocket. Who are you working for? Who pointed you in my direction?'

'Get lost.'

'Take your hand from your jacket. Drop both of them to your sides where I can see them.' When nothing happened, she pulled back the hammer.

The click did the trick.

'Turn around, slowly.' When he was facing her, she pushed the tip of the muzzle of her gun hard against his lips. 'Open. Open your mouth, or I will shoot.'

He parted his lips, 'No, please....'

She pushed the nozzle an inch inside his mouth, and as he tried to protest, she wrenched off his jacket and let it fall to the ground. Then she stepped back. 'Now Mister Jones, or whatever your name is, I have just taken three thousand, eight hundred dollars from you, you fucking old bastard. Not bad, hey. It looks as though you have met your match. Now, whoever you are working with, will want his money back. What will he do when he finds out you cannot give it to him? Shoot you, perhaps?'

'Call me Jones' was very pale and very quiet.

'You are a very good conman. The two of us could be good together. Let us work together and make some money from this man.'

He thought about this and worked out his options. 'He is too powerful. He will kill us both.'

'Ha. So you are not working alone. What is his name? Tell me.'

He went silent again.

'Do you think I will not kill you? You will be my fourth. The last man, I slit his throat, then walked away with two hundred and eighty thousand dollars' worth of diamonds. Just think, if we worked together, all those dollars.'

He took a deep breath. 'Haan.'

'Haan?'

'Albert Haan.'

'How do you know Haan?'

'I help him out, when he's in New York on business.'

'Is he here, now, in New York?'

'Call me Jones' shook his head. 'No, he's in Germany. We corresponded by....' The blast of the Colt 1862 cut him short. He died instantly.

She scanned the area and then emptied the contents of the jacket pockets onto the ground. No gun, or anything that would identify him, whoever he was. She threw what was there, along with the jacket, as far as she could into the river. Then she rolled the body into the water and watched it disappear ahead of a swirl of blood into the muddy depth. A last look around, plenty of gulls but no humans, and left the scene.

Notes on Chapter

Chapter 8

As Frida made her way home, a name pecked away at her thoughts… Neumann. A shiver ran down her spine as she considered the implications of making an enemy of such a formidable businessman. Haan had been the go-between in her dealings with Neumann back in Berlin, and Haan had been the one who had recommended Charles Becker, but that was long before the diamonds. Coming after her without Neumann's knowledge made sense. Unless Neumann knew about the diamonds?

Whoever had been pulling Jones's strings was likely to continue to harass her, somehow or other. Initially, he, or they, would spend the time looking for Jones on the assumption he had double-crossed them, so she had some time to prepare… but for what?

The house was empty. Freddy's room still brought a tear to her eye, but he'd made his choice, and she would have to get used to the idea of not having him around. She paced the property; it needed securing. One or two hidden weapons would be a good idea.

She took pen to paper. *Heinrich Neumann and his employee, Albert Haan, seem to be taking an interest in my wellbeing in New York. If you hear of anything, please let me know. One, or both, employed a conman to swindle me, and I'm trying to find out who's behind the move. Please, Sophie, I shall be forever grateful if you could look into this. Let me know of Neumann's and Haan's movements. Inform me by telegraph if you get news of either of them coming to New York.* She considered sending it to Berlin by telegraph herself, but openly using Neumann's name could cause her more problems. She added to the letter: *If you use the telegraph, refer to Neumann as 'the man'. Haan by 'his man'. P.S., I hope you are well, and be careful.*

Princess returned home with Nathan and Courtney. The girl was still angry with Frida over Freddy's departure, and relayed her day strictly and politely, employee to employer. Frida had assumed that things would return to normal with Jones out of the picture, except, of course, the girl did not know what had unfolded. 'Princess, Jones will no longer be visiting.'

If indifference could be written across a face, it would be across Princess's.

'Princess, he was a conman. I knew all along. You won't be homeless.'

The girl looked at Frida long and hard before speaking. 'Me being homeless is a sad thought, but only a small sad. People like me don' live in a place like this forever an' I am happy while it lasts. Princess is sad about the way you treat your frien'.'

'Freddy? Freddy had no faith in me. He should have known better than to poke his nose in my affairs.'

'But he is broken-hearted.'

'You know where he is?'

'Yes, Ma'am.'

Frida waited.

'Flophouses, mostly on East Side.'

Frida sighed. 'Princess, I had no choice. Jones was not stupid. He was a good con artist. He would have seen through Freddy or you within seconds if you knew it was me who was conning him. Go, see Freddy, tell him I am sorry, and if you must, plead with him to come home.'

'I'll try. Are you sure that man ain't coming back?'

'He will not be coming back.'

The following day, Frida made her way to Broadway, summoned by her lawyer and the firm's private detective, a Brian Wafer. The lawyer, an old, unfit, and dour fifty-year-old, sat at the working side of the desk facing Frida, while Wafer sat sleuth-like in the corner of the room. Frida was there for news of Haus Fischer.

'Your Fischer has surfaced in Boston, coming from nowhere to purchase a four-thousand-dollar property.' The lawyer selected a sheet of paper using a forefinger. 'We have his address here.'

'And you are sure it is him?'

The man nodded. 'Pretty much. German, late forties. Fits your description. Brian has been sniffing around.'

She turned to the detective.

'He offered cash for the property, first thing, but when the law firm told him they preferred a bank draft, he went and opened a bank account. The man has no history, and while that ain't unusual these days, there's a chance that he's who you say he is. He's been at the place for a few months.'

'What name does he go by?'

'Ludwig Rostock.'

The lawyer took over from the detective. 'I assume you are going up to Boston to see this man? Would you like Brian to accompany you?'

Frida shook her head. 'No. I shall not go. It is my close friend, who still lives in Berlin, who wanted to know where her husband had run off to. I shall write to her and let her know.' She smiled at the disappointment radiating from the two men.

A marriage issue. No fortune to be made there. Had they known!

'Gentlemen, thank you for your efforts. My friend will be extremely grateful. I will settle my account on the way out, if I may.' She stood, then. 'One last thing.' She pulled her Colt from beneath her jacket. 'I understand I need a permit to carry this.'

The lawyer flinched. Then laughed. 'That's correct. That's a heavy thing to carry around. You should try....'

'It's also effective. And I can manage it. But can you get a permit for me?'

'What is your purpose for needing it?'

Frida looked at him.

'I'll think of something. I'll let you know when we have it.'

She arrived home making plans about a trip to Boston, wondering if Neumann had news of Becker, now going under the name of Ludwig Rostock. Was Neumann even looking for Becker? She was greeted by Nathen and little Courtney.

'Mama.' Courtney held up a clutching hand towards Frida. Nathen quietly sat on the rug.

'My little darlings. Where is that naughty Mama?' as she kissed both children. 'Princess.' She called up the stairs. The girl's bedroom was tidy and Freddy's room untouched. Frida's room, the basement, nowhere! Princess was nowhere in the house. No notes. Frida stood and stared from her bedroom window... something serious was amiss. Faced with the dilemma of needing to look for the woman and looking after the children, Frida flopped onto her bed. She came to her senses at the sound of hungry cries. She needed Freddy.

She fed the children, then mounted both into slings and pounded the close streets and the market, asking everybody and anybody had if they'd seen Princess. With no luck, she then made her way to the headquarters of North German Lloyd shipping company and asked for Freddy Drich. They sent the request to the back offices.

Word came back to the counter, 'Sorry, Ma'am, he isn't working today.'

Frida didn't believe them. 'Tell him Princess has vanished without taking Courtney. Tell him I am very concerned.'

'Ma'am.'

'I know he is here. Relay this message, and if he still refuses to come out and see me, I will leave.'

The man hesitated, then turned and nodded to the messenger, who disappeared again.

A few minutes later, Freddy appeared. He looked like the old Freddy, dishevelled and nervous.

'Freddy. Have you seen Princess?'

He shook his head. 'Not for a while.'

'She has gone, left Courtney behind. There was no message. I think something has happened to her. Freddy, please, I'm worried for her.'

'I, I can't help. I have work to do.'

'Freddy. Princess is more important than your work. Please help me find her.'

Freddy chewed his bottom lip and fixed his gaze on the woman with two babies on her hips, as though she were a stranger. 'I'm sorry...' and turned and walked away.

Flabbergasted, Frida stood speechless, rooted to the spot, until the man behind the counter cleared his throat. She turned slowly and walked from the offices.

She needed help to find the girl, but where to start? The black shanty town where Princess used to live! If Princess wasn't there, there might be others who could find out where she had gone. And employing somebody from there would be a better option than employing the likes of Brian Wafer. His speciality was white people. She needed somebody to care for the children while she went for help. However, she didn't feel comfortable doing that. She called in at The Astor House and spoke to two of the chambermaids who knew Princess and told them what had happened.

'Miss, that don' soun' right.'

'Do you know the place where she used to live, the shanty town looking over the North River?'

'Yes, Miss. We both still live there.'

'Do you know somebody who can help me find her? I know they will do it for nothing, but I will pay them for their time.'

'That's mighty fine of you, offering to pay, but this is our Princess who could be in trouble. However, we're confident that your generous offer will be gladly accepted. Dollars is hard to come by for the likes of us. You take them babies back to your home an' wait there. Someone will knock on your door tomorrow.'

Frida waited, pacing impatiently back and forth when Courtney and Nathan didn't demand her attention. Struggling to sleep through the night, the following day was long and tiring. Mid-afternoon, a short, plump, well-dressed black woman appeared at the door. She introduced herself as Rose.

'Come in. Come in.'

The lady took a seat on one of the easy chairs and sat looking slightly uncomfortable. She smiled at the children. 'My, my, Courtney, you are growing big and handsome.'

'You know Princess?'

The lady held her head upright in an aloof manner. 'I wouldn't be here if I didn't.'

Rather puzzled by her attitude, Frida asked. 'Have you heard anything?'

'If I had, that girl would be here now.'

'Rose, why are you being so aggressive? Princess is my friend. I want you to find her.'

'Miss. White folks is nothing but trouble, and, from where I'm sitting, you look white all over. I don' need to be your friend, but you have asked the right person to help you.'

Frida sighed. She didn't need this. 'Okay. I do not care if you like me or not. All I need you to do is find that girl. I'll pay however much it costs. Use all the help you need to do it quickly.'

Nathan chose that moment to burst into tears, and Courtney rolled over onto his knees and stroked the baby's cheek. The sight of the black boy comforting his white brother seemed to shame Rose and her white people hatred, especially as Nathan found consolation and his tears stopped.

Rose gasped. 'God has rebuked me.' And she crossed herself. 'Of all the wicked things I've done in my life, He has chosen this moment to put me in my place. It will be my priority... I will find this girl and return her to her infant child.'

Taken aback by the woman's change of attitude, 'You will keep me updated at all times?'

'Yes, Ma'am.'

Frida left the room for five minutes, returning with a silver tray crowded with a silver teapot and two china cups and saucers. She poured. 'How can I contact you?'

'You can come see me or send an errand boy. My place is on Delancey Street, Rose's Bar.'

'You own a bar?'

Rose hesitated, pouring two teas as she seemed to think about her reply.

Frida, a little surprised that her guest took it upon herself to serve, waited.

'I don't actually own it. A man named John Morrissey is the man with his sign on the papers. But he ask me, long time ago, to look after the place. He says the city need a place for black men to get some comfort. He says, treat it like you own it, and make me some money.'

'And you...'

'No Ma'am. Ain't many men fancy the comfort of someone like me, even them black ones. I jus' keep things in their places.'

'I've heard of John Morrissey. Do you know him?'

Rose huffed. 'Not now. That man grows bigger than his body, an' that's big. No, he don't have nothin' to do with the likes of me, just sends his boys round to collect the profits.'

'So, how are you going to go about your search for Princess?'

'It is already under way. I know black men from all the black shanties, and white men from all over Five Points and East Side. If we can't find that girl, no one will.'

'Do you need money? I can get you cash.'

'Princess comes from that same black shanty town as I grew up in. I know that girl from my visits there. Never forget your roots, you never know when you might need them. That girl is in need of her people, an' we don' need your cash. But thank you for offering.'

'Well, if you do… need cash, or anything I can help with….'

Rose smiled and finished her tea. 'Well, I need to go an' continue the search. Come on, Courtney, time to move.' And she made her move towards the boy.

Notes on Chapter

Chapter 9

Frida sprang between Rose and Princess's baby.

'Move aside, woman.' Rose raised the back of her hand, ready to strike, but before she could land any sort of blow, Frida's Colt appeared in front of the black woman's face.

Frida snarled in German. 'One step closer to that boy and this will splatter your brain all over the wall.'

Rose, despite not understanding one word, understood the menace. She lowered her hand but remained frozen to the spot. The nozzle, unwavering and steady, inched closer to the bridge of Rose's nose. Mesmerised, her eyes crossed involuntarily, right until metal touched skin. Frida's thumb cocked the weapon, and the sudden metallic click jolted Rose out of her trance. She backed away. 'What you doin', woman?'

'Get out of this house.' This time in English. 'You find this boy's mother, or it will be you who everybody is looking for. Understand?'

The woman huffed, took a last look down the bore of Frida's gun, and then turned towards the door.

'Find her! Or don't come back.'

'I won' be coming back to this house, ever, you crazy woman.'

She sounded like an older Princess. Frida sat back down and uncocked the gun, anger still streaming through her veins. Two small pairs of eyes stared at her, and the fury melted away.

Unsure whether anybody was looking for Princess, she decided to give it a couple of days, see if any news materialised. It must be time to feed the boys... taking care of them came first, she needed to get organised. Taking care of the house and the boys were Princess's domain. Frida didn't feel confident, and these things were time consuming for somebody who had never partaken in childcare. Much easier to look down the sight of a gun at a woman's face or shoot a man between the eyes than it was to organise the daily routine of running of a household.

However, she managed. With a child on each hip, she shopped. Stall holders recognised Courtney and Nathan and enquired after Princess, and Frida spread the word that the girl was missing. She sang to the boys as she swept and washed diapers. Laid across the rug and played with them. And talked and talked as she walked the streets of Chelsea and Greenwich Village, buying food and looking for Courtney's mother. Not a word for weeks.

She heard from Berlin. Neumann was busy getting himself elected to the Landtag. Sophie Luxemburg still had her ear to the ground after taking over Frida's old information brokerage. She was sure she would have heard of any visiting or dealings with America. Albert Haan seemed to have disappeared into the ether.

Just like Haus Fischer.

Frida stomped about the house, frustrated that Becker was cashing in on her diamonds. But what could she do about it? *Why oh why did you have to disappear now, Princess*? How could she get to Boston while these babies needed her?

The lack of adult interaction was taking its toll. The drudgery of cleaning and caring only added to her burden. As the days grew shorter, Frida spent more time lounging in bed, making any effort only when the children needed her attention. One chilly November morning, she awoke to the harsh glare of the autumn sun piercing through the bedroom window. At last, waking without the help of the boys.

Her body felt heavy as she slid her legs over the side of the bed and sat up, rubbing the sleep from her eyes. 'Morning, you two rascals. Thanks for the sleep in.' She lumbered over to the window and pulled back the drapes, uttering, 'Morning, New York.' As her brain awoke, the silence struck her. Her head cocked to one side and her brow furrowed. She crossed to the cots. Empty.

Confused, she looked about the room. Had Princess returned? She climbed the stairs and checked Princess's room. Then Freddy's. Frantic now, she rushed down to the ground floor… no boys, no Princess. Everywhere, deadly quiet. No open windows, the doors locked.

She threw a coat around her shoulders and stepped out into the already busy street, ignoring the cold on her bare feet, haranguing workers and shoppers as they passed. 'Have you seen my boys? Have you seen my boys?'

Finally, she returned to the house. Realisation struck her. A wave of despair overwhelmed her, and she crumbled to the floor. She ran her hands over her stomach, across her breast. Nathan! Part of her had gone. Taken. She had no idea of how long she sat. Eventually, she hauled herself to her feet and readied herself for the search. She knocked on every door in the neighbourhood, telling all of the abduction of the nine-month-old baby and his almost two-year-old black friend. Pleading for help, and many rallied to the call. Some visited local places of worship and missing persons organisations to spread the word. One man, a newspaperman, promised that his journal would place a notice, seeking information. Frida offered a reward. She visited a printing shop and ordered posters, and called in at her lawyer's office and employed the services of Brian Wafer, the private detective. Then, towards the end of that terrible day, she went to Rose's Bar, along Delancey Street.

The place didn't look like a bar. It was a rowhouse, albeit a big rowhouse. Across the top of the door, a sign, Rose's, just about visible in the gas lit night. The door was locked, and she banged hard. An inquisitive black man's face appeared as an odour of stale tobacco and whiskey escaped into the big world.

'Rose?'

He pulled the back the door and Frida walked in.

Rose almost dropped her welcoming lady demeanour, surprised at who had just entered the establishment. She recovered quickly. 'Miss Brant!'

'Where is my child?'

'What?'

Frida pulled out the Colt.

The man closed in but halted as the gun's chamber rolled and clicked. Frida was arriving at the conclusion; the click was almost as effective as pulling the trigger.

Frida walked over to the proprietor and stabbed the nozzle into the woman's breastbone. 'You heard me. Where are Nathan and Courtney?'

Rose backed away from the weapon. 'I have no idea. What do you mean?'

Frida felt the man move behind her, and she repositioned herself to keep them both covered. 'Move away from your desk,' she said to Rose. 'Put your hands where I can see them. You,' addressing the man, 'stand beside her,' herding him using the gun.

'Miss Brant, what are you doing? I do not have your child. Please put the gun away.'

Frida ignored her. 'My babies have disappeared. This morning. You wanted to take Courtney.'

'Princess's child has gone?' and she raised a hand to her mouth in shock. Without asking, she returned to her chair and sat, ignoring the threat of the gun. 'Please Miss Brant, lower that thing. Somebody has abducted your child… I had no idea.'

Frida lowered the weapon. 'Have you looked for Princess?'

'I had a gang of boys hunting high and low for that girl. She has vanished. They ran out of places to look. Now, they keep an eye out and an ear to the ground. But, I promise you, Miss Brant, they clean run out of places to look.'

Frida nodded, and believing the woman, turned to leave.

'Miss Brant. Allow Daniel to walk you home. New York is no safe place for a woman alone, even someone like you, this late at night.'

Frida turned and scrutinised the man, then nodded, accepting the offer. 'Thank you.'

'Miss Brant, I will do everything I can to help you find your boys.'

Frida couldn't sleep, and the moment daylight arrived, she continued searching, harassing the printer and checking the churches and the charitable organisations. She sought public gatherings, mingling, widening the search.

The next morning... and the following days, her quest for information never relented.

Christmas came and went. 1869 arrived with its wintery welcome. The only thing keeping Frida in the world was hope. February 14th arrived. Nathan's first birthday. She checked his cot, then broke down in a flood of tears. When she had recovered sufficiently, she dragged herself downstairs to get coffee, and to ready herself for another day of disappointment.

Nothing startled Frida anymore. Not even the woman cowering in the parlour. She halted and scrutinised the stranger. Was she here with news of Nathen?

'Who are you?'

The woman gulped. She looked petrified. 'I. I am Martha.'

Frida stared at the stranger.

'My name is Martha. I have news of your boys.'

Frida was kneeling in front of her in a flash. 'What news. What news? Tell me.' And she grabbed Martha by the shoulders.

'He has them. Please don't hurt me.'

The woman's face was grimy, tear-stained. Scrawny and harassed. Almost a mirror image of Frida. 'I will not hurt you. Tell me this news.'

'He has them, your boys.'

Frida's whole being exploded with feelings of hope. 'Who is he? Where?'

Martha shook her head vigorously. 'I don't know. I don't know him. I don't know where they are, but he has them... with my Mary.'

'Your... he has your daughter?'

Martha nodded.

Frida's hands shook. She struggled to put the coffee on the stove. 'Tell me about this man. Tell me everything you know about him.'

'I don't know... he is German, or Polish... I don't know. He spoke with an accent. My Mary disappeared over Christmas. The man says he has Mary, and that she will remain safe as long as I do as he says. I've only seen him in a hood and a cloak, like the Klan. He says to tell you, he has your boys as well. If you do as you're told, they will come to no harm.'

'What are we to do? What does he want us to do?'

She trembled violently. 'He brought me here in the dead of the night. Opened the door and pushed me down in this seat. Told me not to move, for any reason, and to give you the message…. Stop looking for Courtney and Nathan, and do as you are told.'

'I keep the door locked.'

'He has a key.

'What is the Klan?'

87

Martha hesitated. 'White soldier gangs from the South, carrying on the war and still killing.'

Before Frida could ask more, the door opened, and a man waltzed in. Frida jumped up to face him, and Martha burrowed into the seat.

The man, large, unkempt and foul smelling, walked straight over to Frida, grabbed the front of her gown in a clenched fist and growled in an Irish accent, 'You're a mess, lady. Get yourself, the bitch on the chair, and this place cleaned up. Be respectful to your guests. Do that, and those kids will live.' He violently shoved her, and Frida smashed against the wall, pain shooting from the back of her head. He then turned to Martha. With the power of a bear, he ripped off her underwear and raped her, in front of a gaping Frida. Her handgun lay beneath the window... but then... what would happen to Nathan? She buried her face in her hands. Powerless. When the brut had finished with Martha, he coolly belted his trousers and turned back to Frida, walked over, opened her gown, and gripped a breast. With his face so close she could smell his skin, he bit his bottom lip and uttered, 'You'll be my next.' Then he left, leaving the door open behind him.

Martha, crying, curled up and humiliated in the chair. Frida, hurting and shaking uncontrollably, not through fear but with rage, pulled her gown together, forced herself across the room through the horse shit now littering her floor, to the door, and slammed it shut. Martha trembled violently. Frida lowered herself and wrapped her arms around the poor woman, whose tears turned into uncontrolled sobs, and held her tight for a long time, trying to work out what to do.

What could she do? Nathan was alive. That's what the man said. That's what Martha said. 'Martha. We need to stay strong. Can you do that, for Mary? We must do as he says. Get the place clean, get ourselves clean.'

'Where is your washroom? Do you have one? I need it, please.'

Frida led her up the stairs to the top of the house, where she held Martha's face in her hands, gently wiping a tear away with a thumb. 'Get yourself cleaned up and respectable. We need to get through this together. We will get our children back, somehow. I promise,' and kissed her forehead.

Notes on Chapter

Chapter 10

They had no idea what to expect. On day one, there was just one visitor.

Frida cajoled Martha into cleaning herself up. 'They will be back. Work with me, Martha. We need to allow them to control us. Do not make it hard for them. Make them complacent. One day, there will be an opportunity. Don't you want to see your baby again? Tell me about her.'

'She is just over a year old. Has a smile like an angel's....' That was all she could manage without breaking down. Despite not knowing Martha, Frida could see she straddled the edge of sanity.

'Where is her father?'

Martha shook her head. She didn't know nor care.

Frida checked herself in the mirror. She looked as good as she had for a while. Just knowing her baby was still alive restored a glow. 'Trust me, Martha. I can be strong. As long as they only fuck us, we will be alright. Do not give them an excuse to do anything worse. Trust me and allow me to take care of you, and somehow, sometime, we will get the better of them. Then we will see our babies again.'

They dusted and swept, tidied the beds, washed dirty linen and hung the sheets from lines strung across the backyard. Frida dressed Martha in some of her own clothes. A similar physique, she looked good. They kept the windows ajar to air the place of the smell of rapists.

The stench of horse shit was the stench of the street, harder to get rid of. They had enough food for a couple of days. 'Stay strong, Martha, for Mary.'

It was a woman in her later years. Late afternoon. 'Call me mother,' as she pushed her way in without invitation.

Frida's eyes followed her as she walked across the floor, surveyed the room and, smiling, sat herself on the rocking chair by the window.

'This will do perfectly.'

'Who the hell are you?'

'It doesn't matter who I am. I told you, call me mother.' She had a bag, and she rifled through its contents and pulled out needles and wool, and promptly began to knit. 'When I've finished this waistcoat, I'll make you both shawls for the little ones.'

The woman did look motherly. However, looking closely, she was clearly younger than she made out. There was a lot Frida wanted to know. 'Why are you here?'

'To introduce myself, dear. And to look after your interests. Men can be so pushy in matters of the flesh. Sometimes they go too far. I'm here to make sure they behave.'

'I can take care of myself.'

'I'm sure you can. But then those nasty people may get the wrong idea, or hear it wrong, and take it out on little Nathen... or Mary.' Her eyes shifted onto Martha. 'No. The men's behaviour is my concern.'

Frida approached the woman and stood in front of her. 'Where are our babies?'

'I have no idea. You are very intimidating, standing like that. Now, back off.'

Frida didn't know why she did it, but she backed away.

The woman dived into her bag again and pulled out a small cardboard box. 'In here is a wonderful herb called

92

silphium. It's an old Greek aphrodisiac, among other things. It's also a very effective in helping to avoid a nasty conception, which, I should think, none of us want. Martha, my dear, make us all coffee, and drop half a teaspoon into each mug. Thank-you.'

'Is it safe?' asked Martha, holding up the box and studying it.

'I'm going to partake in the brew with you. But if you are unsure, don't drink it.'

'You say it is an aphrodisiac as well?'

'It is, my dear, but the effects won't kick in until they have had their fun and are a mile down the road. It confuses a man's thinking. He will just think it was the best fuck he had ever had.'

Frida still stood. 'What gives you the right to come into my home?'

'Sit down, young lady.'

Despite the obvious contempt for the intruder, Frida sat.

'*You* give me the right to be here. Throw me out if you wish. Come on, you're capable.'

Five minutes later, Martha sliced her way through a silent, poisonous atmosphere, carrying three cups of coffee.

The woman laid her needles down on her lap and sipped the liquid, then, 'I am in the same boat as you girls. If I don't do as I'm asked, if I can't get you to do as you are told, consequences will prevail. Now, you are being blackmailed into prostitution. Bishop Simpson maintains there are more prostitutes in this city than Methodists. What makes you more attractive than those hundreds of thousands of night-walkers and waiter-girls?' She placed her mug on the floor. 'What makes you different is being young mothers. When a customer arrives, make him coffee, talk to him about anything. The weather, politics, shopping. Shopping is good, you can get onto the topic of undergarments. Flirt. What he wants is your body. He'll be sitting there figuring how to get onto the subject, and when he makes a move, disapprove but be jovial with it. Make him work a little for his pleasure. But, he must have his pleasure. That's what he's paid out for.' She hesitated to allow her words to sink in. 'Welcome to Satan's circus, girls. Play your part, and you and your babies will get through this.'

Customer! Frida could feel her blood boiling. This bitch will pay when the time comes.

The girls had to make themselves available from five o'clock in the afternoon until three in the morning. 'Mother' would be present during those hours, every day of the week. Outside of those hours, Frida and Martha would sleep, clean, cook, and prepare for the evening. Neither were prisoners in the house, not in the lock and key sense.

They came, the following day, a steady stream of men. Frida and Martha each had to accommodate four every day. The type of man surprised Frida, especially the early evening ones. She found out they were paying five dollars for the privilege of her pleasure. Unbelievable, when he could have received his similar gratification for a dime from a night-walker. These men appeared well bred. Clean, good manners and finely attired. Gentlemen. The first through the door even came with a bouquet of yellow roses. Almost all came bearing gifts. Within a couple of weeks, both ladies, with the help of mother, had become adept actors, skilled at the manipulation of the male species, giving each and every one a couple of hours to remember. Quite a few returned for more. Frida's reward for her endeavours, knowledge. An achievement, considering how much she hated every second in their company. The thought of revenge kept her going.

She needed knowledge. Time was not on her side. Frida was a woman of means. She owned the house where

94

she was being abused in every night, and she had money in the bank. If they, whoever they were, dug a little deeper into her affairs, it wouldn't take them long to discover a much richer seam of gold. So far, in the excitement of stealing children, the pleasure of inflicting so much pain and the forty dollars a night they earned from this venture, they had overlooked this, and Frida did everything she could to keep them happy, and to keep them overlooking it. She wanted to keep her house and her money, and she wanted her baby back. Retribution will come later.

During after-sex pillow-talk, she never found out who 'they' were, but she discovered much about New York's sex industry. In particular, she and Martha were far from alone in their predicament. It wasn't just young mothers; young girls, dwarfs, Orientals... anybody out of the ordinary. They were all performing against their wills. All victims of 'them'. On the pillow, she learnt about the gangs and the corrupt police forces. The protection rackets, the crooked politicians and judges. The no-go areas and the knock-out-drop gangs. It seemed to her that *they* could be just about anybody living in New York who wasn't a victim.

Frida almost always did the food shopping.

One morning, as Frida waited in line at the bread stall on the market, a voice from behind. Her heart leapt... Freddy! But he wasn't friendly.

'I came to see you yesterday. Got to your door. There was a stream of men back and forth through it.'

Frida turned to face him. The disappointment of the way he spoke showing on her face. He should have seen it. 'Freddy....'

He drew back. 'Don't touch me, whore.' The eyes of the world turned toward the two.

'You have no idea,' as she pushed between him and the other shoppers, 'You dare judge me.... Fuck off,' and she stormed away from the stalls.

Freddy raced after her. 'So why the men? Have you run out of money? Believed one too many swindlers?'

She stopped and faced him. 'They have Nathan. If I don't do as they say....' And then she stepped right into his face. 'But what do you care? Weeks and weeks I've waited for you to help me. And you turn up and make pompous judgements about me. Well, you take your fucking American-way-of-life and go back to your mama. I'll take care of my business.' She jabbed him forcefully in his chest. 'I don't need you.'

*

Into the third month of the ordeal, a breakthrough. In the early hours of one morning, a very young customer turned up, asking for Frida. Pleasantly mannered, he sipped coffee and talked about better things in life, of excursions into the American mid west and sunny resorts of France. His talk reminded Frida of Odette. After an hour of chatting, Mother rocking in the background, they retired to the bedroom. There seemed something unusual about her client, who, the moment they entered the room, sat on the bed and beckoned Frida to do likewise.

'Frida. Sit. Sit.'

Frida, used now to much eccentricity, did as she was asked.

Her visitor took her hand. 'Frida, I have not come to abuse you. I work for an organisation, a charity, out to expose the corruption sweeping New York. I have news of your child.'

'Nathan. Where? What? Tell me.'

'Shush.' He held a finger to his lips. 'We know where he is, and we plan to raid the establishment and release him.'

Frida held back a scream of delight. 'Where is he?'

'I cannot say.'

'You don't know?'

'I…. Yes. I do know. But I've had instruction not to tell you, in case you jeopardise the operation.'

'What if it goes wrong?' Frida couldn't bear to consider the consequences. 'You must tell me.'

The man sat silent for a while, then, 'I'll tell you, but you must promise not to take matters into your own hands.'

'I promise. Tell me. Please.'

He rubbed his beardless face, considering, and as Frida was about to press him harder, '312, on 39th. But you must promise to stay away. This is an opportunity to make a difference in our city.'

Frida slowly nodded, reluctantly agreeing.

'We plan to make a move next week.'

'Next week!' She stood and paced the room. 'I cannot wait until next week.'

'You must. You know what they'll do to your son if they find out you know. They are evil, torturous criminals with no morals. Please leave it to us.'

Her entire body stirred with a thousand emotions. There was no way she could wait. She looked at the man, or more accurately, boy, and wondered how he could have become entangled in such a violent world. Did he expect, or want, what he had paid for?

As if he read her thoughts, 'I shouldn't leave too quickly. You're from Berlin? Tell me about that city, how you ended up here, in New York.'

Notes on Chapter

Chapter 11

Freddy had left behind clothing in a trunk in Martha's room. Frida crept in, and without waking her warn-out friend, had dressed and was ready to go within minutes of mother leaving at the end of the shift. She knew the risks, walking the streets of this city, alone in the early hours.

But this was about Nathan. Her baby.

Every ward had its resident gang, and 39th Street, being on the edge of twenty, bordering twenty-two, would no doubt have two groups of vicious criminals on the hunt for victims. Any law-abiding citizen was a potential target, but during the time of the day when witnesses were non-existent, it wouldn't only be their valuables at risk. Frida packed the Colt for easy access, stashed two six-inch knives in her belt, left the house, and walked northward.

As she turned into eighth avenue, she almost tripped over a drunk man, prostrate and delirious on the sidewalk. He stunk of vomit and urine. His coat, a brown Ulster Coat, looked suitably filthy and well worn if a person wanted to look like a penniless down-and-out. She pulled it from his back and threw her own over him. She also took his hat, a suitable accessory to accompany the coat. She no longer looked affluent, or like a woman.

Thirty minutes later, she stood outside a store displaying filthy rolls of linen that surely nobody in their right minds would purchase. Darkness shrouded the place, and its occupants, Nathan, Courtney and Mary, would be tucked up in bed.

She tried the door. Turned the knob… it was unlocked. The street behind her was moonlit and empty. She listened for danger from beyond the opening, but all she could hear was the thumping of her heart. She pulled the gun from her belt and gently pushed the door open and slipped into a musty room, blacker and colder than the night outside.

As she waited for her eyes to adjust, she felt the hardness of a pistol barrel press into the back of her neck, just beneath the rim of the hat.

'Drop the weapon.'

They had been waiting for her. Her heart plummeted to the floor with the gun. A match flared, and a lantern illuminated the room. It was as it smelt. There were three of them. The two she could see had unkempt beards and wore coats and hats matching those she had taken from the drunkard. The one with the gun on her neck swung her around and pushed her against the wall and shoved his face so close to hers that she couldn't make out his features, other than the smell of his beard. A free hand frisked beneath the coat and the two knives thrown to the floor. It continued wandering, hunting for hidden weapons.

She took a sharp intake of breath. 'You won't find anything there, you bastard.'

'You never know.'

The accent? Faintly German? She could sense the smirk as he stepped back. For half a minute, which seemed like an eternity to Frida, they stood in silence. All three looked like the Irish, but that accent?

The one on the left was the lantern holder. On the right, the dirty bastard holding the gun. The one in the middle… the left sleeve of his coat hung empty. He spoke. 'You couldn't help yourself, could you?' The words were German.

'I didn't think our countrymen could stoop so low.'

'That's good, coming from a Brant.'

Now she was confused.

'Don't get your hopes up. We're not here to save you. But we do know where your boy is, and there is a way you can get him back.'

These men were toying with her, gaining some sort of satisfaction from her pain.

'Those stupid Negros, in possession of all that wealth. They have no idea. But we have. If you want to see your son, we can trade.'

'Trade what?' as if she didn't know.

'You own your house, and you are wealthy.'

She laughed contemptuously. 'You are so wrong.'

He ignored her. 'You can keep the house, but we want five thousand. Then you get an address.'

She shook her head. 'Peter Neumann owns my house. I have no money, other than what he sends me four times a year.'

The one-armed one nodded to the gun-holder, and he slammed his fist into her stomach.

Frida dropped to the floor, gasping for breath.

'Who is Peter Neumann?' and he nodded to his attack-dog again.

This time, it was a kick to the head. Then darkness.

When Frida regained consciousness, dawn had replaced the darkness, and the men had gone. She spat blood as she rolled onto her knees, crawled over to a wall, and sat. Propped against it, she waited for some strength to return. Her Colt and knives lay on the floor, and she pulled the gun to her and closed her eyes. It was past mid-day when Martha eyed Frida struggling along the sidewalk towards the house. There was no coat and hat. Instead, there was a huge black bruise and a vicious cut on the side of her head.

Martha cleaned Frida's wound, forced some hot broth into her and put her to bed. The patient slept through the afternoon and the night. Martha expected business to continue as normal, but five o'clock came and went with no sign of Mother or any men. It was the first night without men for more than three months. The next night was the same. By the third, both women, but especially Martha, began to fret. Their situation had changed for the better, but where did that leave their children?

Two weeks like this passed. Waiting, wondering. 'I don't know how to say this.'

Frida looked at Martha.

'I sort of miss that old woman sitting on the rocking chair.'

Frida understood. 'I do not miss her, but I would like to get my hands on her.' She didn't want to admit it, though. Life had become dull. She missed the constant influx of men, living on the edge of violence. This ordeal would not be over until Nathan was back in her arms and her craving for revenge satisfied.

A few more days dragged by. Frida was alone. Martha had begun to take long daily walks. Things had to get back to normal, she said. Frida agreed, but for her, walks would not accomplish normality. Then a knock at the door.

'Fräulein... Brant?'

Frida looked at him, wondering if it had started again.

'Fräulein. May I enter?'

Frida stood aside, and he crossed the threshold. 'How can I help you, sir?'

He coughed nervously, unsure of himself. 'I am here with news of Freddy Drich.'

Frida's face showed only mild interest, but inside, her heart leapt. However, she would not allow herself to be bitten a second time. 'Is he well? Is he....'

'Freddy has found your child.'

Frida studied the man. He seemed genuine. Normal. Confused at her reaction, or non-reaction.

The scar on the side of her forehead hadn't healed completely. 'Look at this, sir,' and she placed a finger on it. 'The last time I received news of my son, I ended up with this.'

He looked at her. 'Please. Let me say what I have to say… without being overheard.'

'We are alone. Take a seat and tell me more.' Her heart screamed for news. 'My friend is out walking. She will not be back for a while. Would you like coffee?'

He shook his head at the coffee, but took a seat.

'Now, you were saying. Freddy has found my child. Why isn't Freddy here?'

They sat facing each other.

'Freddy explained to me how dear you are to him, and how he messed up your friendship. He understood, too late, that you were in big trouble. The poor boy took it upon himself to help. He watched your place for weeks, until he worked out where these men were coming from, where they handed over their dollar before making their ways here. One place was Rose's.'

Frida stared at him.

'But Freddy needed to find out where Nathan was, so he watched and watched, until he figured who was collecting money from the brothel, you know, not there to see girls. He followed the man to a house next to a concert saloon on the corner of Canal Street and Hudson, a narrow house with a blue door and boarded-up window.'

Frida shook off her mistrust and reached out and grabbed the man on the leg. 'And my baby?'

'Your baby is inside with Courtney and a little girl.'

'All safe?'

He shrugged. 'All unharmed. They seem unharmed.'

Frida went to stand.

'Please Fräulein, hear me out.' He laid a hand on her hand. 'Freddy confronted the man, foolishly. He turned out to be a man not to mess with. He beat Freddy and left him for dead, but, miraculously, he didn't die. But he's in a bad way.'

Frida pulled back and her hand went to her mouth. She hadn't had to think much during the last few weeks. Now, Nathan… Freddy!

'Will… will he live? Where is he?'

'I think so.' The man had a short greying beard and combed hair, looked as though he cared for his looks, but with little success. But he had a sad look in his eyes, eyes that were sad for Freddy's predicament. 'He's in Bellevue. In Manhattan. The doctors there say he'll never walk again.'

Frida didn't say anything, just put her face in her hands. Freddy! Why had she been so cruel? Freddy had been sorry for thinking she was a whore. Had she allowed him to say sorry… apologise? She stood, walked to her dresser and pulled out her Colt, spun and checked the chamber. The noise from Martha's room was overbearing. The man watched her every move.

'Who is this man who beat Freddy? Do you know his name?'

He shook his head. 'I know little about him, other than he's an Irish thug.'

'Not German, or Polish?'

He hesitated, studying her with inquisitive eyes, then shook his head.

'Sorry Sir, what is your name? How do you know Freddy?'

'Otto. I work with Freddy. He has been living with me since before last Christmas, when he moved out of your house.'

'I thought he was staying in flophouses, that's what Princess told me.'

Otto took a deep breath. 'I have something to tell you. Freddy told me to go careful about how I said it.'

Frida joined him again, beside him on the sofa, expecting bad news about Princess.

'Princess is the one behind all this.'

Frida cocked her head.

'Princess stole your boy and is in cahoots with this man. With Rose and her associates. We don't know his name. Together, they have been manipulating this situation, along with the black madam, Rose.'

'But Courtney?'

Otto puffed his cheeks. 'Freddy's is no longer convinced Courtney is Princess's child. Says he thinks Princess has been playing you, ever since she first met you.'

Frida was stunned. This news unbelievable. 'It can't be true.' She desperately tried to think of something, anything, to back up Freddy's assumption. 'She cared for that baby so much.'

Otto shrugged. 'That's the one thing Freddy can't get his head round. She is manipulating the whole situation you find yourself in. But think about it, if Courtney was her child, how could she leave him and pretend to be dead, or whatever?'

'Sir. Otto. Thank you for telling me this, but I must go now.'

Otto stood. 'Can I be of help?'

Frida studied the man for a moment before deciding she would be better off alone. 'Thank you, sir. You can help by staying here until I return. Martha will be back soon. She went to the bureau, pulled out a sheet of paper and wrote…. 'Give this to Martha. It will help. Tell her about Freddy, that he is in hospital, and that I have gone to visit him. Do not tell her about the children. The little girl you spoke of has to be her daughter, Mary. Don't tell Martha what Freddy has found out. We don't want to get her hopes up. Just tell her that Freddy's bad from a random beating and is in Bellevue Hospital, and that I'm rushing off to see him. Tell her you are an old friend; she'll make you coffee.'

Frida quickly made herself presentable for the world outside and left, travelling on foot and at a pace. The journey would take about half an hour, time to think. She hadn't questioned Otto about his story. The thought of seeing her son too fantastic to think properly. But now? While it was quite a walk to Canal Street, it was nothing if you were going to see the son you had thought was dead. It was a similar distance to Delancey Street. Quite a walk to spend a couple of hours with a whore. She slowed. Niggling doubts. Beginning to feel fearful, she kept walking at the slower pace, constantly checking behind, nobody following. Were they still playing games with her?

She found the house with the blue door and the boarded-up windows. The urge to barge in and see her son was strong, but she forced herself to stay calm. She found a shadowy corner opposite and watched across the wide street, thinking about Otto's story. Doubts were resurfacing.

Frida found the strength to wait. Hours passed. It wasn't a white Irish thug, though. She recognised the man who banged on the blue door, Daniel, the black man who had walked her home after visiting Rose. The door opened... and before him stood Princess.

Notes on Chapter

Chapter 12

Frida saw red. That bitch is about to be so sorry. No. Calm yourself. Stay in control. Relish the moment. Remember the babies.

Princess called over her shoulder and another man appeared, the bastard who raped Martha, on that first day... Nathan's birthday. Frida will never forget his face. The two men stood in conversation on the sidewalk, then briskly walked away together. Frida crossed the busy street, her right hand gripping the Colt beneath her cloak, and banged on the door. Princess opened it, probably thinking it was her man returning, completely unprepared for the person standing there. She tried to slam the door on Frida but was much too slow.

In a single flowing move, Frida shoulder barged the door, throwing Princess against the wall. Before the girl could react, Frida smashed the butt of the gun into the surprised face. There was nowhere for the black girl to go, and Frida continued her onslaught, smash after smash around the head, forcing her victim to the floor, then, sitting astride the woman, continuing the beating long after Princess lost consciousness. Long after she stopped breathing. Finally, Frida took a breath, sat up and looked around. Three small faces looked back. Two, standing against the bars of a cot, and Courtney, sitting in a corner. Frida dropped the gun and wiped her hand, clearing away most of the blood, her brain still swirling from the violence, slow to come to terms that her Nathan was here, looking on, safe, and alive.

As her fog cleared, uncontrolled joy took over. Crying and laughing, she crawled over to her little boy and took him in her arms, kissing his dirty face and squeezing an unwashed body. Nathan burst into tears, joined by the little girl. Mary. Frida picked her up as well and danced around the room with the pair in her arms, Frida singing, the babies crying. Frida didn't care. She had her child. Courtney looked on. Frida caught him in the corner of her eye and lowered herself onto her knees. 'Hello Courtney,' and she shifted Nathan onto her left hip with Mary, making a space for the little boy on her right one. He looked at this *stranger* suspiciously, considered his next move, then jumped towards her and clung to her clothing. All without uttering a sound. All together now, Nathan and Mary stopped crying. It was a moment Frida would never forget.

She looked around for something to clean the children's faces. A jug of water and a bowl stood on top of a chest of drawers. Princess's splattered blood sullied her clothing. She rubbed off or hid as much as she was able. Outside in the street, she hailed a cab and fifteen minutes later, they pulled up in Chelsea.

The celebrations began. Tears and laughter. Even Otto, who hardly knew anybody, joined in. Only the children looked bemused. 'Thank you, Otto. Will you stay for a while? Please.' Otto was happy to hang around. Martha went to the kitchen and rustled up some food for all. All this happiness happened in ten minutes, but Frida knew there was one more confrontation to be had before she could relax properly. She took Nathan in her arms and sat with him on the steps up to the front door and waited.

She tucked the colt deep inside her clothing, hoping not to have to use it, and watched the traffic passing in both directions, talking to Nathan all the time, pointing at donkeys and giant horses and other unusual sights. Martha and Mary joined her.

'Are you sure?'

Martha bounced her little girl on her knee. 'I wouldn't miss this for the world.'

One or two local residents stared at the whores with the babies and remembered that Frida had once had a child who had disappeared. After a while, a buggy came into view. Two men sat behind the driver. One was Rose's man, the black Daniel. The other was Princess's co kidnapper. The buggy pulled up at the sidewalk and the two men stared at Frida and Martha… and the babies. Daniel stabbed the driver with a forefinger, and the vehicle pulled away.

Martha accepted Frida's offer and moved into the Chelsea home. Otto, a widower, did the same, and along with the three children, the household returned to the happy, busy place that Frida thought had disappeared forever. Over the summer and autumn, construction work took place. A balcony to the front of the ground floor. The dining room became the kitchen, and the kitchen transformed into a bedroom for Freddy. From his rear door, he could relax in the backyard, or from the balcony at the front he could watch the world go by. All Frida and Otto had to do was persuade Freddy to join them. He had been a long time in hospital. In the end, Frida ordered him, explaining that he had no say in the matter. By the time Nathan's second birthday arrived, the household had settled, and Frida could return to thinking of the future. And the diamonds.

Freddy wheeled his chair onto the balcony and pulled up alongside a thoughtful Frida. 'What are you thinking about?'

'You know what. I am going to have to take a trip to Boston.'

Freddy nodded thoughtfully. 'You be careful. You've got away with killing two people, but none of us wants you to end up in prison. Even now, I half expect Metropolitans to turn up and arrest you.'

'Who said I am out to hurt him?'

'You have form, Frida Brant. Let's assume, though, you do manage it without spilling blood, and you get the diamonds. What then?'

Frida shifted a little uneasily. 'I have not thought that far ahead.'

Freddy knew she was holding back from telling him about her plans because he wouldn't like them. He needed to put other arrangements in place, in case the household faced a future without Frida. And he told her.

'Thanks for the show of confidence.'

'I'm sure you'll do whatever you have to do, and we'll all be fine... but....'

Frida stood and placed herself behind Freddy and stroked his hair with her fingers. She leant over his shoulder and kissed the side of his face. 'I do love you, Freddy Drich.'

*

Haus Fischer had taste, it seemed. The property stood in a spacious plot of land on a residential tree-lined street overlooking a huge lake. Frida looked down at the note, double-checking the address, Jamaica Plain. The sun shone, and women strolled, many in pairs, shading their faces under parasols. Some pushing perambulators. A slight breeze kept the temperature at a perfect level. It was all very peaceful, and Frida imagined the blast of a Colt 1864 disturbing the tranquillity. A dog barked in the distance! Frida exhaled and sat herself against the trunk of a beech tree, perfectly placed to keep her eye on Fischer's house. Just after mid-day, a girl appeared at the door. Plain looking, wearing a maid's uniform that didn't do her justice, and ambled carefree down the road. Easy to follow.

Frida guessed Fischer would employ German staff. She eyed the girl's every move, keeping her distance, then chose her moment. In a dry goods store, she made contact. 'Do you speak German? I'm looking for flowery drapes.'

The girl turned, smiling a friendly smile. 'Yes. Does it show? Do I look *that* German?'

'No. not at all. I'm new here. German is all I speak. I have yet to master the American language.'

'English. You're new in America? I don't recognise your accent.'

'Yes, arrived a few days ago. I come from Schwerin, near Hamburg.' Frida added, 'My name is Ruth.'

'Hello Ruth. I'm Esther.' And they struck up a friendly conversation. Esther asked. 'Would you like a coffee?'

'I would love a coffee; you are not working?'

Esther giggled. 'I should be, but the master of the house,' spoken with open contempt, 'is away for the day.'

Tables populated a lawn beside the wide cobblestone street, served by a small tea-room. The pleasantness of the surroundings, almost overwhelming; young families picnicking at the water's edge, the shiny horse-drawn carriages, the fresh air… so different from the hustle and bustle of the foul-aired New York. Frida didn't like it, and she realised at that moment, she had become a city dweller. It had taken nearly five years, since leaving the small market town of Schwerin.

'I take it he's German,' said Frida, making herself comfortable. 'What about his wife?'

'He's not married. Too many bad habits. He's probably drunk in some brothel or another in the city as we speak. He proudly and boringly tells us he's a Berliner, and that's how real Berliners live, almost every evening when he comes home worse for wear. Who would want to marry that?'

'Why do you work for him?'

'Because he's an idiot. He's mostly away during the daytime, and he's unmarried. There are two of us in the house, the cook and me. It's a very easy life. The worst part is his flirting, but he's normally drunk enough for us to laugh it off, and I can tell you from experience, it's better than working for some bossy lady of the house.'

'Do you live in the house? Sleep overnight. I wouldn't be happy with somebody like that lurking around while I slept.'

'No, never. He sleeps late anyway. It suits him that we can both be on hand in time for his breakfast. It is an undemanding job. No wife, no children, no animals, no visitors, although he tells us his mother might join him soon. I suppose that will be the end of our little utopia.'

Esther hailed from Berlin, and Frida knew of many of the places they spoke about, and they spent a pleasant hour together, talking about Esther's dreams of her future in America and memories of the old country. The girl could talk.

So, Fischer would be alone this evening. And drunk, with a bit of luck.

*

Frida watched the two women walk away from the house, down the street after their day's labour, busily talking to one another. Fischer had been home for about an hour, unsteady on his feet as he climbed onto the stoop. She bet the man would be dozing by now.

The door was unlocked. She crept into the large hallway and stood, listening in the murkiness. Fischer's grunting and snorting drifted through a doorway. He slouched on a comfortable chair with wide padded arms, the fingers of his right hand locked around an empty crystal whiskey glass. The half-full bottle sat lonely on a low table beside the chair. Frida crept behind Fischer and topped up the glass.

'Fischer snorted, 'Who's there?'

'It's Esther, Ludwig.' She whispered.

'I thought you'd left.' And he sleepily sipped his golden nectar.

Frida stood until he forgot she was behind him. He seemed to be dreaming pleasant dreams as he rhythmically raised the glass to his lips until it was empty. The man was sleeping contently now, no longer drinking. There was little light, just enough to study the room. Frida refilled the glass and raised it to his lips. Fischer half opened an eye and gave a surprised grunt. Then continued sipping.

'Ish that you Esther?'

'I'm here Ludwig.' She whispered back.

'You're my best girl, better than that....'

'Drink up Ludwig.'

And he drank. Frida knelt behind him and gently blew on his neck, just behind the ear. 'You're my favourite, too. I love a man who loves his whiskey.'

'I love my whiskey.'

'I love the way it sparkles through the glass.'

'I love the way you sparkle,' and he chuckled.

She kissed him tenderly on the ear and he shuddered. 'Drink up Ludwig.'

He upended the glass. All gone.

She refilled it.

'I cud make... I cud... with you.'

'You would make me sparkle.'

'I cud make you sparkle, I cud. You wud sparkle like diamonds.'

'Oh diamonds. Ludwig. Diamonds would make me love you and love you, my darling. I've never seen a diamond.'

'I cud show you…'

'I would like to feel diamonds on my naked skin. I want to show you diamonds against my naked skin?'

Half-an-hour later, Frida crept from the house, thirteen diamonds gripped fast in her hand. Ludwig Rostock, Haus Fischer, sleeping like a baby.

*

Freddy couldn't believe how she had managed it. 'One missing though.'

'I know. I almost cut his throat in revenge.'

'So. Now what?'

Frida changed the subject. 'You would like Boston, Freddy. Especially Jamaica Plain. The roads are smooth, the air fresh. It would be a good place for the children as well.' She told him all about the lake and the picnics and the street-side cafes. 'I think, when I've solved the problem of changing the diamonds into cash, we could all move there.'

Freddy smiled. It sounded like a nice dream, but he would put it on hold for the time being.

Notes on Chapter

Chapter 13

As the household settled, Frida had too much time to think, and most of the time revenge dominated those thoughts. She craved revenge. The identity of everybody involved in forcing her into prostitution and kidnapping Nathan had to found, then she could put her plan into action. Rose and Black Daniel must suspect that Frida would not let their past misdemeanours go unpunished, that eventually they would pay. Patience wasn't a strong point, her consolation was imagining the pair looking under their beds in fear every night. Princess's thug had done a disappearing act, and she was confident Black Daniel would eventually lead her to the low-life, and probably others involved. There had to be another, more local, establishment whose owners or staff took the five dollars and sent men on to her. Rose's was too far away. The one-armed thug at the store on 39th had said that the racket was being run by Negros. But he was German. He may have had nothing to do with their predicament, but he knew about it. And despite seeing his country kin in trouble, he had planned not to help but to take advantage of the situation. She instructed Otto to keep an ear open. That German and his compatriots were on her list.

In addition to her dark ambitions she still had a quarter of a million dollars' worth of stolen diamonds to fence. She took Otto's arm and together they perused New York's nightlife, searching the gateway into the city's seedy underbelly. She had done some research, scanning newspapers and journals, and the vast majority of businessmen and public servants exposed for corruption hailed from the Irish-American tribe. So they headed for Broadway and Park Row. Much of it was too intimidating. Otto put his foot down, and Frida didn't argue. All the brothels and many of the bars were no place for a female, even chaperoned, but she enjoyed the hotel lounges, where she overheard lots of political, business and even organised crime gossip. Her favourite places, though, were the concert saloons, and Harry Hills was her very favourite. Houston Street on the corner of Bowery, a popular attraction for its variety shows and concerts. A busy place where, eventually, every politician, actor, businessman, stock exchange trader and run-of-the-mill scoundrel passed through. Her first visit coincided with a demonstration by moral reformers targeting perpetrators of indecent and disorderly conduct. It hadn't lasted long, and soon she experienced the reasons behind the protest. She loved it. But she loved the waiter girls the most. They were wicked. Every man's eyes popped out when they danced, especially the French can-can.

By day, the place could be mistaken for an aged wreck, but by night, a place of non-stop gaiety, lit up by a huge lantern and a band that never stopped, a dance floor constantly packed and waiter girls in red-tasselled boots and low-cut dresses swirling around carrying drink-laden trays.

On that first visit, Otto and a laughing Frida pushed their way toward the bar. On stage, a line of waitress-dancers danced, kicking their legs high in unity and whooping in time, dresses struggling to keep the troop dignified. Otto's eyes bulged. They ordered whiskeys and Frida wished Polke could be here.

Somewhere, in amongst this crowd of high spirits, existed a portal into the world of black money. The couple returned, week after week. They came, they drank, they laughed, and they danced. Slowly but surely, Frida got to know who was who in New York's world of politics, business, and crime.

On a morning of swirling fallen leaves, Black Daniel made his way north along The Western Boulevard and stopped at a small bar just two hundred yards from Union Street. It wasn't a black man's drinking place, and his kind would not normally have been welcome. However, he stayed long enough to down a beer. The following day, Frida sent in Otto to make enquiries about some young-mum whores.

'They told me the place was no longer in business. It had been good while it lasted, and it had been a shame it ended. They hoped Rose would get her act together and find another. However, seeing my disappointment, they suggested an establishment specialising in young, clean, willing kids. Fifteen dollars. Ten-years-old! The way they talked, a man could buy just about anything.

Frida placed the bar on her watch-list for the next few weeks. Two men visited regularly, together, once every week on the same day. Short and stocky brothers, with thick folds of their necks bulging over their collars. She had seen them at Harry Hill's. Frida had got to know a talkative individual named O'Connor, a somebody in the days of the Dead Rabbits, a notorious Irish American street gang in New York City of the 1840s and 1850s. They were one of several gangs that operated in the city during that time, primarily breaking skulls in the Five Points neighbourhood of Lower Manhattan. What O'Connor didn't know about the workings of the underworld of the city would fit in a matchbox.

'The pair has a round, a collection of bars, shebeens, saloons, and brothels, who pay for protection. They answer to Hill, Harry,' he threw a thumb over his shoulder, 'who in turn answers to Morrissey.'

'Morrissey?'

'Well, the Tammany. Same thing.'

Frida was about to ask about 'the Tammany', but Otto nudged her with his knee.

'That's how it works. Make a donation to Tammany Hall, and you place won't get smashed up, and if you get arrested, well, you got protection there as well.'

'What about Rose's Bar?'

'What about Rose's Bar?'

'Well, she tells me that Morrissey owns the place.'

O'Connor wiped his mouth with his sleeve. 'That's the thing about Morrissey. If owns the place, he takes the profits. If he don't own the place, he takes most of the profits.' And he laughed.

'How do I speak to John Morrissey?'

O'Connor guffawed.

'Well?' prompted Frida, annoyed at the put-down. 'How?'

O'Connor stared at the German woman standing in front of him, and the embarrassed Otto standing beside her. 'Are you Irish? You don't sound Irish. You don't get to speak with John Morrissey unless you're Irish or a Democrat congressman.'

'Or somebody with money?'

O'Connor, realising the woman was serious, sighed. 'I'll see what I can do.'

Freddy wheeled his way into the parlour. 'What on earth were you going to talk about? Surely not the diamonds.'

She laughed. 'Do you really think I'm that much of an idiot? No, I want to join his Democrat Party. Associating with their kind might bring about an opening. It's worth a try.'

'Umm. Could be.'

'It's Otto's idea,' she lied.

Freddy immediately changed the subject. Frida smiled to herself.

She waited a few weeks, but the loudmouth never came back with news of any meeting. He didn't get anywhere... or didn't try. Frida maintained her surveillance on Rose and Black Daniel, and the bar along The Western Boulevard. It was there that Princess's thug one day poked his head above the parapet. Obviously, a friend of Jack Delany, the bar's owner. Known as Big Mike, the man rests his head nightly at a dosshouse near the docks at Corlears Hook.

Freddy joined her in the backyard. Frida stood leaning against the back wall. 'Aren't you cold out here?'

She smiled. 'I needed some air. That bastard, O'Connor, hasn't got back.'

'You really thought he would? He's Irish, you're German. They don't mix. Never have, never will.'

'You're right, but it's a shame. It was worth a try. I'll have to come up with another way.'

*

There were four long rows of tables in S. Heim's Café. Packed rows, except for the chairs either side and opposite Frida Brant; the whore from Union Street. S. Heim's Café was a mile or more from Frida's house, but the German community who frequented the place all thought they knew about her past exploits. The oompah band blasted out its loud, lively music. With steins of lager held high, the clientele rocked their bodies from side to side in rhythm. Frida was doing her best to enjoy herself, but the isolation from being shunned made it difficult. All around, laughing and singing. She could handle being ignored. It was the whispering cow sitting a few places down, unable to hide her animosity, who threatened to push Frida over the edge.

The approaching men were on a mission. Stern faces and rigid neck muscles signalling their intentions as the two made their way towards her, barging between rows of swaying backs. Frida's heart rate increased. She felt the blood throbbing throughout the veins, the backs of her fingers twitched. She was frightened, not of the men, but of her rising anger and the damage it might lead to. The Colt felt heavy against her ribs. But she was Frida Brant, and as fearful as she was of her looming reaction, she couldn't bring herself to leave. To give any of them the satisfaction of seeing a Brant in flight.

Her skin crawled as the two of them sat down beside her, one on each side. The sounds of laughter and the music became a muffled hum as her hearing tuned in to the voice of the management's lackey. 'We don't want your sort in here.'

She closed her eyes... *Don't touch me.* Frida could feel them preparing to manhandle her out of the establishment. Her heart slowed, and she stopped breathing.

'Fräulein Brant...' as his fingers wrapped around her upper arm.

Frida's elbow struck him in the eye and her hand slipped inside her jacket... and a mug of beer slid across the surface of the table, coming to a standstill in front of her.

The grips loosened, the one on her arm, and the one around the handle of the gun. Three pairs of eyes looked across at the individual who had launched the mug, the face more familiar to the two men than to Frida. The pair dropped their heads, stood and backed away. No words. Frida squinted. The face was hard and menacing, and Frida's mind raced, trying to place it. It... looked... familiar. She had seen it before. Slowly, a glimmer. Hasso Schinkel's man. Schwarzblut.

Frida had laughed when Hasso had told her his name. 'I can't call him that.'

'You won't have to. I doubt very much that you'll ever meet him.'

Frida remembered being puzzled.

'Schwarzblut is a man who is good for just one thing, and that's not socialising. He's my man, Frida. His expertise is killing.

But Frida had met him, fleetingly, when Hasso was teaching her how to use a handgun. Just a kiss on the back of her hand, and he was gone. The light in S. Heim's Café was dim, but Frida could still see into the man's unblinking eyes, dark and bottomless. Scary. 'Schwarzblut.'

The slightest of nods. 'Fräulein Brant.' A hint of a smile. Perhaps a twitch.

'I remember you. Hasso's friend. What are you doing in America?'

'Looking for somebody.'s

Frida waited for him to elaborate, then. 'Who?'

'Your brother.'

Frida didn't reply.

'Stay where you are. I'll join you.'

As he made his way around the end of the row, Frida caught the gaze of the whispering cow. This time, the woman immediately looked away. Frida smiled to herself, and as she did so, she realised Schwarzblut had already taken his seat. The man was light on his feet, considering his size.

'Your brother, Claas Brant.'

'Yes, I know who my brother is.'

'You haven't seen him?'

'If I had, one of us would be dead.'

Schwarzblut seemed to weigh up the sentence, then gave the slightest of nods. 'I've been in America for a year. Here, then Boston, Chicago, Philadelphia. He's

123

disappeared into thin air. I returned to New York one week ago. It appears you've had problems.'

'You know?'

'Yes. I'm sorry I wasn't around.'

'What could you have done?'

'I would have been at your side.'

Frida realised she was being abrasive, and laid a hand on Schwarzblut's, in the way of an apology. 'I'm sorry, Herr Schwarzblut. This crowd has affected my mood. Hasso spoke of you with affection. Where were you when he died?'

'Cholera. While Herr Schinkel died and they forced you away from Germany, I couldn't....'

Frida's eyes dropped to the beer in front of her. Schwarzblut's silence was deafening. In no hurry to break it, she raised the mug to her lips and sipped the liquid through the froth. The band had stopped playing, and the air filled with the sounds of Germans enjoying themselves. She no longer felt threatened. It was because of Hasso Schinkel's man. She turned back to him and touched him on an arm. 'Herr Schwarzblut. I would like to leave. I would like you to leave with me.'

Notes on Chapter

Chapter 14

Frida was slowly getting used to it. Whenever they had met, since S. Heim's Café, and despite trying her hardest, she had never seen Schwarzblut approach. It had become a challenge. She laughed when Otto nearly jumped out of his skin when the big man blew in his ear. Schwarzblut nodded to Frida. Big Mike was no more. The man who had crushed Freddy's spine had paid the ultimate price for being such a bastard. Frida and Otto had been waiting for Frida's man on The Western Boulevard, outside Jack Delany's bar.

The clientele fell silent as their eyes turned towards the woman who entered. Just as it wasn't a place for a black man, this bar was not a place for a woman.

Otto led the way through the dim smoky atmosphere. At the bar, he turned to face the drinkers. 'Time to leave, gentlemen.'

'Who says so?' One piped up, speaking on behalf of the twenty or so punters.

'Drink up.' Otto demanded. When Schwarzblut stepped up beside Otto, nobody else protested. They all, to a man, gulped down whatever had been in their glasses and did a fast exit.

Delany, who had been spitting into his whiskey glasses to enhance the shine, lowered his well-used cloth and demanded to know what the hell was going on.

Frida faced the bartender. 'Mister Delany, I have taken over your rental agreement of this property,' and she placed the paperwork on the bar.

'You can't do that.'

'I'm afraid I have. Here is the paperwork,' jabbing the small pile of papers. 'Your license has been cancelled and I am now tenant and licensee. You must leave now. I shall allow you one minute.'

Delany, drawing his skinny self up to look bigger, repeated, 'You can't do that. My stuff.' He jerked his head upwards. 'On the floor above. All my belongings. If you continue with this ridiculous course of action, I'll have you horse-whipped. You don't know who you're dealing with.'

Frida sneered. 'You now have thirty seconds. If you want to carry on living, you had better get moving.'

'I'll make you fucking pay, you bitch.' Delany's handgun lay at hand on a shelf beneath the bar. The eyes gave him away, his intention written all over his face. Frida placed her hand in full view beside the stack of glasses, the fingers clasped around the grip of her Colt. 'I have already paid. All those dollars you took from men who came to fuck me. This is retribution.'

The barman swore again and pulled open a drawer full of dollar bills.

'No you do not. The takings belong to me.'

'You can't do this,' he pleaded. 'I'll be homeless. Penniless on the streets. Please....'

'Times up. Schwarzblut.' And Schwarzblut made a move towards the bar. That was all it took for the Irish Skinball to dash for the door leading onto The Western Boulevard, screaming obscenities with every step.

Frida looked around the large room and instructed Otto to organise labour. 'Get it from Kleindeutschland. Only Germans, understand? Women to clean the place, it stinks, then painters. Get rid of the drink, give it away...

throw it, I don't care, but we can't have that cheap rubbish in here.'

Otto nodded. 'We should put more lighting in.'

'Yeah. And check out the shithouse. I'll leave it to you, Otto. Come on Schwarzblut, we have an appointment with Harry Hill.'

Hill had a body like Jack Delany's. There were lots of them in this city. Mid to late thirties, a product of Ireland's potato famine. A body that, as a boy, had survived those years and had never really recovered from the ordeal, had become used to eating very little, and with a mind not to share. A hoarder of anything that glittered, never to be trusted. Frida could almost see through the thin skin of his face as he welcomed them with a sickly smile.

'That was a very poor decision, kicking Delany out like that. We stick together, us Irish. Take a seat. Let's discuss the situation.' The man spoke only to Frida, no acknowledgment of the presence of Schwarzblut.

Frida remained standing. 'It was justified. The man belonged to a gang who kidnapped my baby boy and forced me into prostitution, threatening my baby's wellbeing if I refused. I had months of being screwed by the filthiest scum in this city, because of that man. He is fortunate only to be kicked out onto the streets.'

'Well, you should have come to us with your complaint, and we could have solved this problem amicably.'

'Well, I did not, and it's now solved. Let us get down to why I am here. Whatever you decide to do with my little bar on The Western Boulevard, I will repay you in kind, and,' she made a point of looking around. 'You have much more to lose than I.'

He looked straight at her, the slightest of grins across his translucent face, a face that couldn't be read. 'I'm a busy man, Ma'am. I hear your words. Remember, this tit-for-tat you speak of would not stop at this saloon.

Anyway, I'm a busy man. Is this what you've come here to say?'

'Rose and Black Daniel, of Rose's whorehouse, were part of that gang. The fourth man, going by the name of Big Mike, is dead. I want Rose and her lackey on the streets with Delany within the next forty-eight hours, penniless and homeless. I am giving you that opportunity to dish out fair justice, but if you cannot, I'll do it for you. The money you skimmed from the bar on Western Boulevard was profit made from the abuse of my body. At the moment, I am inclined to forget about that. However, there will be no more *dues.*'

'You give me too much credit, Ma'am. I'm in no position to carry out your wishes.'

'Well, you clear it with Morrissey, or Tammany Hall, or whoever your paymasters are. As I said, you have forty-eight hours to deal with Rose. It will save us all a lot of trouble if you can do this.' She expected the period of silence. Hill would attempt to make her feel uncomfortable. She never gave the man the opportunity. 'Thank you for your time, Mister Hill.' And she turned and walked out of the saloon, the watchful Schwarzblut following.

'You said that?'

Here we go, thought Frida.

Freddy was just starting. 'Haven't you caused enough trouble for yourself. It's... it's as though you have a death wish. Ever since you got here.'

'None of what has happened has been my fault.'

'Now you plan to take on the Irish. Why take on the bar. Have you got the money for it?'

She was slightly concerned, the venture was turning out to be more costly than she had anticipated. 'You worry too much. Once we open we'll all live like Kings.'

'But why take it on?'

'You know why, Freddy Drich. That bastard Delany sold young girls to the scum of New York. He sold me, and Martha. Him and his likes need to be wiped off the face of the earth. I'm doing this city a favour.'

'You could have done that without buying the bar.'

'Yeah, well.... We need to earn a living.'

Freddy shook his head. 'I'm worried about you.'

Frida ruffled his hair and then gave him a gentle thump on the upper arm. 'There really is no need to.'

*

The workers had taken what they wanted from Delany's bar and apartment. Anything left was burning in the yard. By the time Hill's 'brothers', the two protection money collectors from Harry Hill's concert saloon, visited, the place was almost ready to open. Frida checked her timepiece, forty-eight hours after her ultimatum to Hill, right on the dot.

They waltzed across to the bar in tandem. 'Miss Brant. Rose's bar is under new management.'

Frida acknowledged the news without interrupting the stacking of new glasses.

'Mister Hill invites you along to his saloon to discuss your weekly dues.'

Frida stopped stacking and eyed the visitors up and down. 'You tell Mister Hill to drop in and see me. I will pour him a glass of the finest Irish whiskey, on the house. He can do that on a weekly basis, if he desires. It is the only due he will get from me.'

The brother who had spoken nodded in acknowledgement. It didn't seem as though he had expected to hear anything else. Both turned and left.

Frida sighed with relief as they walked away, and double-checked that her gun was handy and ready for use. She sensed eyes on her and looked up to see Schwarzblut standing at the foot of the stairway. She smiled. The first room at the top of the stairwell she had commandeered for Otto, his office. The next two, she had given to the giant, no more dosshouses, or wherever he had been laying his head. He had graciously accepted. The other rooms would be for storage. There was a small yard at the back of the premises housing the logs supplying the four roaring stoves heating the place, and tools, such as ladders and wood-working and decorating equipment, and the bonfire of the rubbish. Drinks from German brewers were on their way, due tomorrow. Christmas and New Year's Eve were approaching fast, and next week was Thanksgiving. They were ready for the grand opening this Saturday, and a busy few weeks to follow.

1870 fast approached. New decade. New business. New York. She poured ten glasses of Schnapps and called everybody to the bar. Three men, four women. Today, painters and cleaners. Tomorrow, waitresses and bartenders. She summoned them all. Plus Otto and Schwarzblut. She raised her glass. 'Here's to our new bar, The Little Lady. Put the word around, we open, mid-day, Saturday.'

'Prost!' The others followed suit.

*

The brewers delivered beers and spirits. Frida, Otto, and Schwarzblut played the customers, and the seven Männer und Frauen practiced thier roles. Just after midday, right on schedule, the photographer arrived. After *action shots* of the interior of The Little Lady, Frida gathered them out on the street, to stand below the shiny new sign, and the photographer prepared his camera. Onlookers congregated, to witness the birth of this new venture. Amongst them, to Frida's delight, Martha had somehow persuaded a smiling Freddy Drich to come along.

131

'Ready!' And a flash.

And screams! A group of men with handguns burst out from the crowd and ran across the cobbled street, indiscriminately shooting into Frida's group. Using too much force, Schwarzblut grabbed Frida and threw himself to the ground, wedging her beneath him. Everything was swimming, the surroundings blurred, and then everything went black. Then whistles. Shouting of Municipal Police filled the air as she regained consciousness. Windows cracked as flames licked the glass. The bar was ablaze.

Frida tried to move, but Schwarzblut had her pinned tightly to the sidewalk. 'Let me move, you hulk,' and her lungs filled with air as he rolled off her.

But he hadn't rolled off. Police hands dragged him off. Hit twice, once in the shoulder, and once in the back of the head, Schwarzblut had died. So had Otto. And one bartender and two of the waitresses; a father and two mothers. The other waitress lay badly injured, and one bartender had a bullet in the arm. Just one bartender and Frida had escaped injury. Frida buried her face in her hands. But not for long.

'Move! Get away from the building!' A policeman grabbed her and pulled her to her feet. 'Move away, lady.' Firefighters rushed past towards a solitary fire hydrant.

Everything was still a blur. She made out the images of Freddy and Martha standing on the opposite sidewalk, both waving, and hobbled towards them, pain shooting across her chest as she did so. She had taken a battering, but she was alive. As the crying Martha reached out, an explosion came from inside the bar. The spirits had gone up. The place soon became an inferno. Firefighters had no chance.

Frida collapsed to her knees and flung her arms around the crippled Freddy. 'I'm so sorry, Freddy. So many people dead. Children. Orphaned.'

'Frida. Frida. Listen to me. You're okay. That's the important thing, for Nathan, Courtney, and for me.' They cried with each other as police laid out the dead and firefighters fought a losing battle against the flames. Frida thought of Odette.

Freddy placed his hands on Frida's face. 'Frida.' Frida sobbed uncontrollably. 'Frida, there is a woman here to see you.'

Frida wiped her face with the back of her hand. 'Where?' She sniffed, 'Who?'

The visitor stood at the edge of the spectators on the other side of Freddy's chair, staring at Frida.

Frida gasped in disbelief. Sophie Luxemburg!

'Hallo Frida.'

A confused Frida stood. 'Sophie. What are you doing here?'

Sophie held flowers. 'Herr Neumann sendet Ihnen seine besten Grüße.' She approached, unsure steps. 'I am so sorry.'

Best fucking wishes! Frida turned her back on the woman from Berlin and watched glowing embers rising and floating across the roofs of New York. Souls of the dead bodies scattered across the cobble-stones... growing cold... and disappearing.

From somewhere, a voice. Don't run my darling Frida. No more running.

Notes on Chapter

Printed in Great Britain
by Amazon

39325797R00076